William Gillette

All the Comforts of Home

A comedy in four acts

William Gillette

All the Comforts of Home
A comedy in four acts

ISBN/EAN: 9783744781602

Printed in Europe, USA, Canada, Australia, Japan

Cover: Foto ©Andreas Hilbeck / pixelio.de

More available books at **www.hansebooks.com**

All the Comforts of Home

A COMEDY IN FOUR ACTS

BY

WILLIAM GILLETTE

As produced at the Boston Museum, for the first time, Monday, March 3d, 1890

NEW YORK
HAROLD ROORBACH, PUBLISHER
132 NASSAU STREET

All the Comforts of Home.

Dramatis Personæ and Original Cast.

ALFRED HASTINGS, *Pettibone's nephew* . . . . MR. JOHN MASON.
TOM McDOW, *a protégé of Alfred's* . . . . MR GEO. W. WILSON.
THEODORE BENDER, ESQ., *a retired produce dealer* . MR. GEO. C. BONIFACE.
JOSEPHINE BENDER, *his wife* . . . . MISS ANNIE M. CLARKE.
EVANGELINE BENDER, *their daughter* . . . . . MISS MIRIAM O'LEARY.
MR. EGBERT PETTIBONE, *a peculiarly jealous man* . MR. THOS. L. COLEMAN.
ROSABELLE PETTIBONE, *his second wife* . . . . . MISS LILIAN HADLEY.
EMILY PETTIBONE, *Pettibone's daughter* . . . . . MISS EVELYN CAMPBELL.
CHRISTOPHER DABNEY, *a broken-down music-teacher* . . MR. CHAS. S. ABBE.
JUDSON LANGHORNE, *a young man of leisure* . . . . MR. ERROLL DUNBAR.
FIFI ORITANSKI, *from the Opéra Comique* . . . MISS EMMA V. SHERIDAN.
AUGUSTUS McSNATH, *a friend of Pettibone's youth* . . MR. JAMES BURROWS.
VICTOR SMYTHE, *in love with Emily Pettibone* . . . . MR. JUNIUS B. BOOTH.
THOMPSON, *a shoe-dealer* . . . . MR. H. P. WHITTEMORE.
KATY, *maid at Pettibone's* . . . . MISS MARY HEBRON.
GRETCHEN, *Fifi's maid* . . . . MISS BLAKE.
BAILIFF, *merely a bailiff* . . . . MR. EDWARD WADE.

WHERE IS IT ?
Drawing-room of a private house in London.

WHEN IS IT ?
Now.

WHAT TIME IS IT ?
ACT I. — A Morning.
ACT II. — A Few Mornings Later.
ACT III. — Another Morning.
ACT IV. — The Same Morning.
(Good-Morning.)

TIME OF PLAYING. — TWO HOURS AND THIRTY-FIVE MINUTES.

"AN' I GITS HALF."

2

Costumes.

ALFRED. Ordinary business suit. Change in Act III. for costume suitable for an afternoon call.

TOM. Grotesque assortment of garments all rather the worse for wear.

BENDER.
JOSEPHINE. } The attire of a well-to-do provincial family on a
EVANGELINE. } visit to the metropolis. BENDER has gray hair.

PETTIBONE. Black frock coat and waistcoat; fancy trousers; overcoat; silk hat; gloves. He has iron-gray hair and mustache.

MRS. PETTIBONE. Act I. — 1st dress, morning-gown; 2d dress, travelling costume. Act IV. — Same as 2d dress in Act I.

EMILY. Act I. — 1st dress, street gown, hat, gloves, parasol, etc.; 2d dress, travelling costume. Act IV. — Same as 2d dress in Act I.

DABNEY. Eccentric and old-fashioned clothes; tall hat, etc., for 1st enter. Dressing-gown, flannels, bandages, etc., for invalid bus. at end of Act II. and in Act IV. He wears a bald wig.

LANGHORNE. Clothes ultra-fashionable and somewhat loud. He carries a small cane and red or tan gloves. Small mustache.

FIFI. Very stylish street costume and house-dress. Comic-opera costume ("Prince Vladimir") at end of Act II.

McSNATH. Ordinary rig of an elderly business man. Light-gray hair and whiskers.

SMYTHE. Fashionable but quiet attire, complete in every detail.

THOMPSON. } Ordinary every-day dress, marked by sufficient ec-
BAILIFF. } centricity to suggest their occupations.

KATY. Maid-servant's costume, with outer garments for travelling.

GRETCHEN. Street dress; neat but plain.

Properties.

ACT I. — Small table up L. Ottoman L. Shelves with books, ornaments, etc., against wall L. Table R. or R. C., with armchair L. of it, and smaller chairs R. and back of it. Upright piano C. or up R. Large mirror up R. Pictures on walls and bric-a-brac around room. Desk L. with chair before it. Other chairs conveniently disposed about stage. Table up stage. Hat-rack up L. C. Carpet down. Key in door R. 3 E. Open letter and watch for PETTIBONE. Satchel, two or three small parcels, and bird in cage for EMILY. Bell on table R. Fan and several small parcels for MRS. PETTIBONE. Books, portfolio, papers, writing-materials, etc., on desk L. Money (in envelope) and keys in PETTIBONE'S pockets. Travelling things for EMILY and KATY. Parcel, rolled in carrying-straps, for ALFRED, to contain cuffs and shirts, etc., showing at the ends; a few books; a pair of fencing-foils; a set of boxing-gloves; a pair of riding-boots; a long pipe and a bootjack. Notebook and pencil for ALFRED. Umbrella, gripsack, and other travellers' articles for PETTIBONE. Two small dogs. Package of bird-seed. Sponge and cake of soap. Pawn-ticket for ALFRED. A painted sign, "Elegantly Furnished Apartments to Let," with the bottom portion broken or. torn off. Crashes overhead; off L. 2 E.; and outside, up L. Two feather-beds, two bolsters, and two blankets overhead. · Water-pitcher and glasses on table up stage. Money for SMYTHE. Bills in pocket-book for DABNEY. Red pigment (blood·) for TOM. Box on desk L., containing two small articles (audiophones) for the ears. Card-case, containing cards, for FIFI.

3

ACT II. — Furnishings, etc., as in Act I. Tray of breakfast things, cup of tea, package, bunch of keys, mustard-plaster, pail of hot water, and sealed note for TOM. Bells off stage up R. ; L. 2 E. ; and overhead. Pipe, tobacco in bag, and matches for BENDER. Dressmaker's bill (L. 3 E.) for FIFI. Hat and cane for BENDER. Jewel-case off R. 3 E. Bundle of legal papers for BAILIFF. Bill for THOMPSON. Money in ALFRED'S pocket. Money, in purse, for JOSEPHINE. Newspaper in ALFRED'S pocket. Table-cover, on table near C., for BENDER to snatch. Mustard-plaster for DABNEY.

ACT III. — Furniture, etc., as before. Large pasteboard box, as per description, page 74, for TOM. Pot of black paint and brush on table C. Bells off stage, L. 2 E. ; and up R. Hook on wall near foot of stairs. Hat and cane for BENDER. Bell, pipe, paper novel, beer-mug, and noise overhead. Hat for ALFRED to enter with. Newspaper. Demijohn, newspaper in wrapper, sealed letter, and two bottles of champagne for TOM. Umbrella off R. 3 E. TELEGRAM. Key for FIFI. Breakfast-hamper containing two bottles of champagne (one a dummy) ; some French chops ; a salad and other fancy dishes ; rolls ; corkscrew ; wine-glasses ; knives, plates, tablecloth, napkins, etc., for two ; also two bunches of flowers for corsage and buttonhole. Fountain pen for ALFRED. Book on table. Vase for BENDER to smash. Crash and step-ladder off R. 3 E.

ACT IV. — Furniture, etc., as before. Table up C. Money in purses, satchels, parcels, and other travelling things used in Act I., for MRS. PETTIBONE and EMILY. Towel about DABNEY'S head. Rugs, umbrella, portmanteau, etc., for PETTIBONE. Lock inside of door I. 3 E. Papers and plaster (L. 2 E.) for PETTIBONE. Dressmaker's bill for BENDER. Paper (used in Act I.) for ALFRED.

Abbreviations.

In observing, the player is supposed to face the audience. C. means centre ; R., right ; L., left ; R. C., right of centre ; L C., left of centre ; C. D., centre door ; R. D., right door ; L. D., left door ; D. R. C., door right of centre ; D. L. C., door left of centre ; D. F., door in the flat ; C. D. F., centre door in the flat ; R. D. F., right door in the flat ; L. D. F., left door in the flat ; I G., 2 G., 3 G., etc., first, second, or third grooves, etc. ; I E., 2 E., 3 E., etc., first, second, or third entrances, etc. ; R. U.E., right upper entrance ; L. U. E., left upper entrance ; UP, up stage or toward the rear ; DOWN, down stage or toward the audience.

R.   R. C.   C.   L, C.   L.

4

All the Comforts of Home.

ACT I.

SCENE. — Parlor or drawing-room in EGBERT PETTIBONE'S *house. A handsome room, luxuriously furnished. Large square or arched opening up* R. C., *through which is seen a large heavy door up* R. *to open on stage, and also the lower part of a winding stairway, leading up, and practical, with balustrade, etc. A door up* R. *near 3, set on diagonal so that it faces toward middle of front of stage. This door has a transom above it to open. The door opens on the stage. Door down* R. *Wide or double doors up* L. C., *to open up stage. Interior backing showing a window (practical), and above this street backing. Door down* L. *Door up* L. *or* L. 3. *Doors* R. *and* L. *are each backed with handsome interior pieces. It is important that the door up* R., *near stairs, should be solid, to slam heavily; and it would add greatly to the effect if all the doors could be similarly built, and the transom over door* R. 3. *Handsome tables, chairs, etc., as per bus. A small table up* L., *either in corner or against wall, to pull out for bus. An ottoman or short lounge* L. *Shelves for books, ornaments, etc., against wall* L., *for bus. (*BENDER *upsetting things,* ACT III.) *Handsome table* R. C. *Upright piano up* C. *or at* R. *A large and elegantly mounted mirror (for bus.) up* R., *either just above door* R. 3 *or up* C. *This mirror may be a part of some large and elegant piece of furniture. Handsomely framed pictures (paintings, etc.) hang on walls* R. *and* L. *and up stage. One or two at* R., *slightly*

5

... figure-paintings, but not too much so. Chairs, etc.,
... back of door up L. C., and furniture of a char-
... nature up above opening up R.

NOTE — *As this scene stands for the evening, advantage should*
be taken of the fact to have the setting very complete in every
respect. Rich, luxurious furniture, cases of books and bric-a-
brac, etc. Handsomely framed paintings, etc., hanging on
walls. Hall up R. Stairs and rooms R. and L. outside of
doors, carpeted with different varieties of stuff, etc.

     MUSIC. — Lively music for Curtain. Continue pp.
     a few bars after curtain is up. READY EMILY,
     to enter door up R.

     DISCOVERED, EGBERT PETTIBONE, *pacing up*
     and down and around room in a very excited state,
     with a letter in his hand. Runs other hand through
     his hair distractedly. Drops into chair; looks at
     the letter; buries face in hands. Jumps suddenly
     up and paces again. Repeats chair bus.

PETTIBONE.   I have suspected it all along! Now it is no
longer suspicion — it is certainty. (*Bus.*) I was cautioned
against marrying a young wife — at my age. Ah! — kind
friends (*agony; eyes up to ceiling*) — kind friends — you were
right. (*Bus. Letter to light.*) I have a copy of her letter
— making the appointment. (*Looks at it. Reads.*) "Come
this afternoon between one and two o'clock. No one will
be here to disturb us!" Oh! (*Bus.*) I have arranged
that! (*Paces about the room, muttering.*) Some one will be
here to disturb you Mr. — Mr. — (*looks at letter*) Victor
Smythe!

     ENTER EMILY PETTIBONE *door up R.; hat and*
     walking dress on, as if just in from street. She
     has two or three small parcels and a little satchel
     such as ladies carry for shopping. She is about to
     pass the wide door of room up R., when her father's

conduct attracts her attention. She comes into the room a little way, watching him, and soon bursts into a merry laugh. PETTIBONE *turns quickly. Crosses to and fro* R. *and* L. *Conceals letter.*

EMILY (C.).   How many laps have you made since breakfast ?   (*Laughs again.   Comes down* L. *of* PETTIBONE.)   Do tell me what is the matter this morning.

PET. (R. ; *goes to and fro and stops* R., *meeting her*).   Matter ?   Nothing !

EMILY (C. ; *peremptorily, but good-naturedly*).   You hid a letter — I want to see it !   (*Bus.*)

PET. (R. C.).   No ! No !   (*Avoiding her.*)

EMILY.   What !   As bad as that !   I shall have to report this to my stepmamma.

PET. (*aghast*).   What !   Report that I — that I — (*aside*).

[EMILY *bursts out laughing again.*

EMILY (L. C.)   Oh — but you're in a state !

PET. (R. C. ; *recovers*).   Ah — e — hem !   It's only business, my child.

EMILY.   Business !   (*Looks incredulous.*)

PET.   Listen !   You have often expressed a wish to travel — to see the world.   (*Crosses to* L.)

EMILY.   Yes ; but you needn't go into convulsions about it, papa !   I can wait a little !

PET.   You will not have to wait !   We start to-day !

EMILY.   Oh ! you dear — (*about to embrace him*) good —

PET. (*stopping her*).   No !   We haven't time for that ! (*Crosses to* L. *and* R.)

[*READY* KATY, *to enter door up* L. C.

EMILY.   Goodness !   You must be in an awful hurry !

PET.   Hurry ?   I am in a — (*stops in midst of rising rage ; aside*).   No — no — no !   She must not suspect.   (*Aloud.*) Emily, my dear (*kisses her, but in an excited and mechanical fashion*). I am suddenly compelled to go to the Continent

…an business of vast importance.　I shall take you and — and your stepmother with me.

EMILY (L.).　Oh!　That is simply heavenly!

PET. (R.).　You have only half an hour to get ready!

EMILY.　Ready now — walk right off with you — only want to throw some things into a trunk.

PET. (R.).　Your trunks are packed.

[EMILY *now surprised.*

EMILY (L.).　Dear me, Popsy, but you are in a hurry!　And Katy —

PET.　I told her to put in everything she saw.　(PETTI-
BONE *rings bell violently, on table* R., *dropping it, etc., in excitement.*)

EMILY (*aghast*).　Everything she saw —　Mercy!

[*READY knock and voice up* R.

[*ENTER* KATY, *door up* L. C.

PET.　My daughter's trunks — are they packed yet?　Are they packed, I say?

KATY (*up* L. C.).　Yes, sir — they are, sir.

PET. (R.).　And — Mrs. Pettibone — her trunks — our trunks — ?

KATY.　They're all ready, sir — but she doesn't understand why —

PET. (*suddenly forgetting himself*).　Eh!　(*Eagerly.*)　What did she say, eh?

KATY.　She said it was her opinion, sir, as you was gone completely crazy.

PET.　She's right!　I — e —　Go and tell her she's right, do you hear?　(*Fumes about.*)

KATY.　Yes, sir!　　　　　(*EXIT* KATY, *up* L. C.)

[EMILY, *who has been watching* PETTIBONE, *bursts
into laughter.*

PET.　Do!　And if she wants to know — (PETTIBONE
stops suddenly and looks sheepish).

EMILY (L.; *solemnly, shaking finger at* PETTIBONE). Popsy — there's something at the bottom of all this!

PET. (R.). No! (*Shakes head emphatically.*) Nothing at all, only business. (*Turns* L., *shaking head, muttering about business, etc. Paces out into hall up* R.)

[*Knock outside*, R.

READY MRS. PETTIBONE, *to enter up* L. C.

(*Calling off* R. D., *to someone.*) Is that the cab? Is the cab there, I say?

VOICE (*outside*, R.). Yes, sir; and the men are here for the luggage.

PET. Send them up the other way. The other way, you fool!

VOICE (*outside*, R.). Yes, sir.

EMILY (*starting*). Mercy! I must see if Katy has put in everything — and my bird — and, and — oh, dear! (*Runs off, up* L. C.)

PET. (*coming down* R.; *looks at watch nervously as he paces*). Now, why doesn't Alfred come! I sent word from the office an hour ago that he must come at once — and it's long after that now. He must stay here in the house — he can't object — far better quarters than the little garret where he's lodging now. And I must let him know that I approve of his suit with Emily — and I must give directions about the house. Confound it! (*Paces.*) We haven't fifteen minutes — and — all these things to be settled! (*Crosses* L.)

ENTER MRS. PETTIBONE, *up* L. C. NOTE. — Mrs. PETTIBONE *is very deliberate and cool, a contrast to the others.*

PET. (*comes down* R. C.; *aside*). Ah — my wife — Now for it! (*Goes* L.) Have you attended to the packing, Madam?

MRS. PETTIBONE (*sits* L. *of* R. *table; chilly tone*). Oh, yes — I have nothing to do but attend to your orders.

PET. We are about to start on a — a little trip.

MRS. P. (*stops fan bus.; looks at* PETTIBONE). Ah! When do we go, pray?

PET. (*watching her narrowly*). We leave — this morning.

[MRS. PETTIBONE *starts slightly.*

(*Aside, quickly.*) She started!

READY ALFRED, *to enter up* R.

MRS. P. (*aside*). Poor Victor! He will be heartbroken.

PET. (*aside; watching her*). She is thinking of the appointment! I can see it!

MRS. P. (*aside*). He must overcome his impatience until we return.

PET. Come, come! It is nearly time. Your things — Your — your — (*Stops as he meets her gaze. Crosses* R.)

MRS. P. (*rising and crossing up to* L. C. D.: *looks calmly at* PETTIBONE; *walks leisurely to door up* L. C.; *turns*). I suppose it has not occurred to you to tell me where we are going — whether to Asia, Africa, the North Pole, or the Sandwich Islands?

PET. (*Crosses up to* C.). I — I — You will know before — before —

MRS. P. Before I get there? That would be delightful!
(*EXIT up* L. C.)

[PETTIBONE *stands speechless, looking after her.*

PET. (L. C.). Oh — you are very composed! Yet I saw you start once — and — and this letter — this letter! (*Grinds teeth.*)

ENTER ALFRED HASTINGS *up* R., *carrying a parcel rolled in carrying straps — cuffs and shirts, etc., showing at the ends; a few books; a pair of foils; a set of boxing-gloves; a pair of riding-boots; a long pipe, and a bootjack.*

(*Seeing* ALFRED.) What in the name of common-sense kept you all this time? I said at once! At once!

ALFRED (R.). Kind and severe uncle and guardian, you did.

But you also ordered me to bring all my belongings, as I was to stay here. These orders of yours clashed. My landlady objected to the removal of my property.

PET. (L.). Then you left it, of course?

ALF. Oh, no; I brought it.

PET. Those?

ALF. These. (*Puts things down on table* R.)

PET. Is that all?

ALF. No; I have quite an assortment of pawn-tickets in my pockets. (*Sits luxuriously* L. *of* R. *table.*) It's the best way to have property — a fellow can move so easily.

PET. (L.; *starting suddenly*). Well, we have no time to talk. (*Becomes more and more excited.*) I am starting on a journey with my family.

ALF. (*slight surprise*). Don't say!

PET. Yes. You are to stay here and take care of the house. No one is to know where I am going. Not a soul — not a soul.

ALF. Well, where is it?

PET. I — haven't made up my mind.

ALF. Devilish good idea! So long as you don't know, I don't think anybody else is likely to discover.

PET. If they do — if he follows us — (*Bus.*)

ALF. (*after watching* PETTIBONE *quietly, rises*). Let me feel your pulse. (*Bus.*)

PET. Nonsense! Don't interrupt me — we have only four minutes. Now, as to my daughter Emmy. You love her — don't interrupt — I know it — it's all right — you have my consent.

ALF. By Jove! (*Bus. as if to seize* PETTIBONE's *hand.*)

PET. (*pulling away*). No — we haven't time for that! (*Goes to desk* L., *nervously. Bus. with things. Throws papers about excitedly.*)

ALF. (C., *aside*). Gave his consent — but doesn't know what he's saying. I'll make him put it in writing. (*Scrawls*

quickly on note-sheet. Aloud.) Sign this. *(Going to Petti-
bine, L.)*

Pet. *(reading).* What is it?

Alf. Your consent. You might die — I think you will.

Pet. (L.). Well, well! *(Scrawls his name on the consent.)*
You are not rich — but I can trust you.

Alf. Thanks. So can I.

Pet. It is said cousins should not marry — that their
children are liable to be lunatics. Nonsense! Perfect
rubbish!

Alf. Nothing in it.

Pet. Nothing. *(Laughs derisively.)* Ha, ha, ha!

Alf. Absurd! Ha, ha!

Pet. Ridiculous! Ha, ha, ha! Simply ridiculous!
Why, look here! My own parents were cousins them-
selves!

Alf. *(stops laughing; aside).* By Jove! There's something in it after all!

Pet. (L.). Now, listen! I will tell you why I leave town
so suddenly. It is because my wife *(grasps Alfred's sleeve;
hisses in his ear)* is deceiving me! She is false! False!

Alf. (C.). Now you're wrong, Uncle, believe me!

Pet. "Believe me!" Don't I know? Oh! I have overlooked a good many things. Dudes and coxcombs paying
all sorts of attention to her — confound them! *(Bus. Rushes
up and down L. Stops before Alfred again.)* But now I have
proof — proof, I tell you! I have seen a fine gentleman lin-
gering near for some time — following us to concerts, thea-
tres, operas, — always getting a seat as near as possible.
There have been looks exchanged — there have been letters
written —

Alf. (R.). The deuce!

Pet. (L.). Ah! you begin to see! *(Paces excitedly.)*

Alf. No, sir; I don't see anything!

Pet. *(vehemently; first glances L.).* Then, look! See some-

thing ! Her letter ! Making an appointment — here ! Two
o'clock ! "No one to disturb us !" Ugh ! Read ! Read !
(*Paces about room.*)

> [ALFRED *looks at letter, and gives a whistle.*

(*Starting*). Ugh ! Don't do that — read — read !

ALF. (R., *reading*). " My dear Mr. Smythe : I will grant
you the interview you ask. Come this afternoon between
one and two o'clock. My husband is at his business then,
and no one will be here to disturb us. You must be very
cautious, however, or you will spoil all. Yours ever, Rosabelle Pettibone." (*Turns it over.*) This is in your handwriting, I observe.

PET. (L.). Yes — I copied it; and then I sent the original
on. He will get it ! He will come ! His name is Victor
Smythe, d —— n him — and there will be some one here to
disturb him !

ALF. Of course. You will wait and fight him !

PET. Fight ? That is what he wants — to put me out of
the way ! No, sir ! I am going to surprise him ! He will
find you here to receive him !

ALF. Jove ! You surprise me !

PET. And you must give him a reception that he won't
forget. (*Doubles fists and pantomimes.*)

ALF. I must, eh ? (*Smiling bus.*)

> [PETTIBONE, *bus. of sighing vigorously.*

(*Laughing.*) All right. I'll attend to the gentleman.

PET. You will ?

ALF. Certainly ! Delighted — dislocate his nose. (*Bus.*)

PET. (*delighted*). That's it !

ALF. Knock out an eye.

PET. (*bus.; enthusiasm*). Good ! Ha, ha !

> [*READY* MRS. PETTIBONE, *to enter* L. C.

ALF. Lacerate an ear

PET. (*bus.*). Ha, ha ! Yes ! Ha, ha !

ALF. Do him up generally.

PET. (*bus.*). Do him up! Ha, ha!

ALF. Then — to avoid unpleasant results — tell him it was all a terrible mistake — wrong man — apologize — sew up his ear — set his nose — write a prescription — and charge him five pounds.

PET. Ha, ha! You're a nephew after my own heart!

ALF. (R. C.). No! It's your daughter's heart I'm after.

PET. (C.). Yes! I see! Ha, ha! [*Both laugh.* (*Suddenly.*) What! (*Watch.*) It's time to start! Merciful powers! Suppose the fellow should find me here! (*Rushes L. C. Calls off.*) Here — Emmy! Rosabelle! Hurry! Hurry! (*Dances back to* ALFRED. *Bus. of getting things from pockets.*) Here — money — carry you through this month. I'll send more soon. Take good care of everything — keys. (*Bus.*) Look out for this one — key to wine-cellar. (*Crosses L.*) [*READY* EMILY *and* KATY, *to enter L.*

> *ENTER* MRS. PETTIBONE, L. C. *She is in travelling costume. Carries several parcels, and is buttoning her glove.*

MRS. P. (*down* C.). Ah, Alfred! I suppose you have not heard that we —

PET. (L.). Yes, yes! He is to live here and take care of the house. If any one comes, he will receive them!

> [MRS. PETTIBONE *starts slightly. Crosses to* L. (*Aside to* ALFRED — *quickly.*) Did you see that?

> [ALFRED *nods.* MRS. PETTIBONE, L. PETTIBONE *picks up overcoat, hat, etc., up* C., *still keeping his eye on* MRS. PETTIBONE.

MRS. P. (*aside*). If I could only get word to him not to come!

PET. (*down* C.). Come, come! No more delay! (*Up to* L. C., *and calls.*) Emmy! Emmy! (*Up and down* C., *glancing excitedly at* MRS. PETTIBONE *now and then.*)

EMILY (*outside, L. C.*). Coming, papa! Coming!

MRS. P. (*to* ALFRED; *approaching*). Your uncle seems to be having some kind of a fit to-day.

ALF. (R.; *aside*). A mis-fit, I should say.

ENTER EMILY, L., *with travelling things, bird-cage with bird, etc., followed by* KATY, *also prepared for journey, and leading pug dogs by strings, or carrying them.*

EMILY (*down* C.). Here I am — and (*sees* ALFRED). O Alfred! Good-by! (*Holds out her hand to him.*) Did you ever hear of such a sudden start?

ALF. (R.; *to* EMILY). Your father has consented.

EMILY (C.). What!

ALF. (R.). Look at that! (*Shows paper.*)

EMILY. He's crazy! (*Gives* ALFRED *a look. Crosses to* R.)

[PETTIBONE *and* MRS. PETTIBONE *have filled time with bus. of getting ready.*

PET. (*down* L. C.). Emily! You don't intend to carry the birds! And your dogs, Rosabelle —

EMILY (R.). But how could we leave them, with no one to take care of the darlings?

PET. (*going to* D. *up* R.). Didn't I say that Alfred is to stay here?

EMILY. Oh! (*Bus.*) Then you shall take care of my little birdies!

MRS. P. (*taking dogs from* KATY *and hurrying* L. *to* ALFRED, *who is* C.). And my darlings! I'll trust them to you, Alfred! (*Giving them to* ALFRED.)

EMILY. There are the seeds. (*Getting them from* KATY *up* C., *and down* R. *of* ALFRED. *Putting packages in* ALFRED'S R. *hand.*) And you know about the fresh water every morning? (*Bus.*)

PET. (*near door up* R.). We must go, I tell you!

[*Both ladies exclaim, and hurry toward door up* R.

MRS. P. (L. *of* ALFRED; *bus.*). They must have a walk every day — and no meat! And — (*getting sponge and soap from* KATY.)

EMILY (R.; *to* ALFRED). And if their feathers come out —

MRS. P. Oh — and the bath-sponge and soap — the dog soap — (*putting it under* ALFRED'S L. *arm*).

EMILY. And green things. Come, mamma!

> [PETTIBONE *calls. All call good-by', etc., and EXE-UNT door up* R., *leaving* ALFRED *loaded with cages, dogs, and any truck that can go with them. READY* TOM, *to enter up* R.

ALF. Good-by! Good-by! (*Bus. of following them to door, waving dogs, bird-cages, etc.; stumbling about.*) I'll take care of everything! (*Turns and goes across to* L. *after bus.*) I'll give these things a dose of arsenic. Here — they can just go in here for the present. There you are! (*Etc., to fill out bus.* ALFRED *puts poodles, birds, etc., off at door* L. 3. *Surveys the place.*) This isn't so bad! Uncle Egbert's jealousy may be deuced annoying to him, but I don't mind it in the least. An elegant mansion at my disposal — not to speak of the key to the — (*smiles*). Now, if I could only think of some way to raise the money for old Hiflin's note that comes due to-morrow, I'd be perfectly serene. As I can't, I'll be serene anyway. Let's see — he didn't leave me enough to — (*looks at contents of envelope*). No — oh, no — bare expenses. I — oh, by Jove! I forgot all about Tom. (*Goes into room up* L. C., *and opens window back. Speaks off.*) Hello, there! Tom! Come in; you'll find the door open! (*Shuts window and comes down.*) I can give him a lodging now; that'll help the poor chap along a little, anyhow. Heaven knows I'd give him money if I had it; he's had a hard row to hoe. (*Sits* L. *of* R. *table luxuriously in easy-chair, half reclining. Smokes.*)

> ENTER TOM McDow *up* R., *stopping uncertainly at entrance to room.*

Hello!

TOM (*down* C.). Gee-whiffles! This ain't the place, is it?

ALF. (*seated* R.). Yaas — I've decided to take the house for a few months, although it isn't quite up to what I wanted.

Tom. Holy smoke ! You must 'a' struck it rich !

Alf. Thomas, this is my uncle's house. He has gone abroad with his entire family. I am to stay here and look out for things. You are to stay and look out for me !

Tom. Yes, sir. (*Looks about.*) What shall I go at first, sir ?

Alf. Well, the first thing required is to entertain a certain gentleman named Victor Smythe, who is expected to call here between one and two. Thomas, remove my raiments. [Tom *takes* Alfred's *traps off table* R., *puts them into room* R. 2 E., *and returns to* C.

(*Raises himself a little absently, feeling for watch. Pulls out pawn-ticket. Bus.*) Ah ! My watch is being — 'hem — regilded. (*Reclines again.*) No matter. We can tell the time by Smythe. When he comes it'll be about one o'clock.

Tom. Will we receive him with honor, sir ?

Alf. (*still seated* R.). Eh ? Oh, yes ! We will honor him with one of the most scientific thrashings known to art.

Tom. (C. ; *putting himself into pugilistic attitude*). Thrashings ? You don't mean — (*motion or two — absently, looking questioningly at same time at* Alfred).

Alf. That is the idea. I've given my word to attend to it — and I trust I can count upon you — to —

Tom. Count, Mr. Hastings ! I'd do anything in the world for you.

Alf. Thanks —

Tom. After your kindness to me, sir, and getting me out of that there scrape —

Alf. That's all right (*waving hand to quiet* Tom).

Tom. And borrowin' the money to do it —

Alf. (*rising up a little*). But I know all about it, my boy.

Tom. And promisin' to take me into your office —

Alf. (*emphatically*). When I have one, Thomas.

Tom. Quite right, sir. And this note that's a-bothering you, Mr. Hastings — if I could only think of some way to fix it — I'd — (*looks about*).   If this was on'y your house, now, we could sell it, couldn't we ?

ALF.   Yes — or let it — and live on the income in affluence and luxury.

TOM (*business of trying all the chairs by sitting on them one after another*).   This here funnitoor an' fixin's would fetch a tidy little pile — an' here we are only two of us to sit in 'em. It's clear waste, sir, that's what it is !

[ALFRED *sits up, and looks around room.*

ALF.   Wait a minute.   (*Bus. of looking, etc.*)   It's all right !

TOM.   Is it, though ?

ALF. (*rises to* C.).   Yes.   We'll let these rooms to lodgers !

[TOM *glances about quickly.*

(*Excitedly.*)   It's one of the most desirable places in town. (R. C.)   Make 'em pay a month in advance, of course.

TOM (L. C.).   Of course — or two months — or a year, sir !

ALF.   No — a month will do.   Then I can take care of that infernal note, and keep out of the clutches of the law. I want you to go in with me on this —

TOM.   I'd do anything in the world for —

ALF.   Yes — I know.   I can't pay you, though — haven't got it.   But I'll take you into partnership, by Jove !

TOM (*doubtfully*).   What'll that do to me, sir ?

ALF.   We go in together, don't you see ?   I run the — er — the business part of it — you take care of the lodgers — we divide the profits.

TOM.   Divide the prof —

ALF.   You get half.

TOM.   I gits — half !   Do you really mean it, sir ?

[ALFRED *nods.*

(*Delighted.*)   Ha, ha, ha !

[ALFRED *laughs also.   Slaps* TOM *on back.*

ALF.   May make your fortune, my boy.

Tom. It ain't that, sir! I don't care for the money — but — ge-whiffles! I gits half! Ha, ha, ha! That's the first time as such a thing ever occurred to me — I give ye my word, it is. (Tom *bus. of hopping about with delight.*) What's to do, sir? Oh — just gimme something to do — quick! (Tom *in his restlessness is near door up* R. *on this speech.*)

Alf. The first thing is to get a sign out announcing lodgings to let; a nicely painted —

Tom. Yes, sir! (*EXIT quickly door up* R.)

Alf. Artistic sort of thing that will attract. Hello, the fellow's gone! (*Looks about.*) This is a clever scheme, by Jove! and he put it into my head. He'll be just the one to help me with it too. He'd do anything in the world for me. Never saw a fellow so grateful as he was when I pulled him through that little scrape he was foolish enough to get into. (*Sits at desk* L., *and writes.*) Now, I suppose some sort of a lease or agreement is necessary — or — let me see — "Rules for Lodgers." That's it! Rules is what I want. First. "Rent must be paid strictly in advance." (*Writes it. Looks about as if trying to think of something else.*) That's the only rule that seems to occur to me. In this case — oh — ah — (*writes*). "Children and dogs" — what is it that children and dogs do? Oh, yes — (*writes*). That settles children and dogs. Here's another. (*Writes.*) "Anything ordered will be charged extra." That doesn't sound quite right, someway; but it'll have to go.

[*ENTER* Tom *quickly up* R.

Tom. (R.). Here it is, sir!

Alf. (L.). What?

Tom. The sign. (Tom *shows a nicely painted sign which reads —*

ELEGANTLY FURNISHED
APARTMENTS
TO LET.

The bottom portion being evidently broken or torn off.)

ALF.   In Heaven's name where did you get that?

TOM.   Just down the street.

ALF.   Buy it?

TOM.   Not much — took it off a house.

ALF.   Good gracious, my boy, that's going too far!

TOM (*breathless*).   Only four doors past the corner, sir.

. ALF.   But, see here — you'll get us into trouble — it's theft, or burglary, or something of that kind.

TOM.   Theft? No, sir.   It says 'ere, "elegantly furnished apartments," sir.   They warn't nothing of the kind — they're terrors.

ALF.   How do you know?

TOM.   I see 'em through the winders, sir; the furnishin's is vile.   An' I says to myself, I'll take down this lyin', swindlin' sign, an' put it where it'll speak the truth, and nothin' but the truth — an' that's on this here house, sir.   An' up she goes — an' I gits half!   (*EXIT, door up* R.)

ALF.   But I say — here, Tom!   He's certainly taking hold of the business with a vengeance.   If he goes on like this, we'll end up with elegantly furnished apartments in the police station.

> *ENTER* TOM *up* R. — *breathless, as from rushing up and down stairs, etc.*

TOM (R.).   It's up, sir — an' they's three parties as stands starin' at it a-ready, with their eyes as big as oyster-shells.

ALF. (L. C.).   But first, as to the rooms.   We'll have to settle how much we're going to ask.

> [ALFRED *goes to different doors, followed by* TOM; *first to* L. 2 E., *passing* L. 3 E. *to* L. C. D., *then crosses to* R. 3 E. *and* R. 2 E.

TOM (*murmuring to himself*).   An' I gits half!

ALF.   It isn't arranged like an ordinary house for lodgings, is it?

TOM.   No, sir, I can't say as it is.   (*Very downcast.*)

ALF.   All the better.

Tom (*suddenly reviving spirits*). Yes, sir. All the better.

[ALFRED *bus. of a look at him to catch this point.*

ALF. More homelike —

Tom (*eagerly*). So it is !

ALF. (*to* C., *back to audience, surveying the room*). Lodgers will have the use of this big drawing-room, with the conservatory and large front windows commanding a view of the park. (*Pointing to front for these things.*) Nothing like it. All the comforts of home. I say, that's a good thing—don't forget it. Give it to 'em strong, Tom.

Tom (R. C.) Yes, sir. Give 'em what, sir ?

ALF. (L. C.). That idea — it sounds well. All the comforts of home.

Tom. Quite right, sir. (*Aside.*) I'll go an' paint it on to the bottom of that there bill — "All the comforts of home."

ALF. (*going up and looking in door up* L. C.). Now, Tom, about prices. This room has an alcove adjoining.

Tom (R. *of* ALFRED, *up stage*). Yes, sir.

ALF. Five pound, ten.

Tom (*repeating to himself joyfully*). Fi pun, ten.

ALF. (*up* L. C. ; *about to write it down in book*). I'll put it down.

Tom (R. *of* ALFRED. *Sudden yell, and bus. of seizing* ALFRED'S *right arm*). No ! don't ye do it — oh, it's worth it — it's worth it !

ALF. Keep quiet. I'm only going to put it down in this book.

Tom (*sheepishly—after staring an instant*). Oh! I thought ye was a-goin' to put the price down.

[ALFRED *goes to door* R. 3, *followed by* TOM.

ALF. Here are two very good rooms.

TOM. Very good rooms, very go —

[ALFRED *turns quickly.* TOM *stops suddenly.*

ALF. Three windows.

Tom.   Three an' a 'alf, sir — you didn't count that there thing. (*Pointing to transom over door.*)

   [*READY knock, and noise of falling furniture and throwing of beds.*

Alf.   That's nothing.

Tom.   Nothing !   It's worth ten bob extra at least, sir.

Alf.   What possible use is the thing ?

   [*READY* Smythe, *to enter up* R.

Tom.   Use, sir ?   Can't the parties as lodges there stand on a chair or table an' git a beautiful prospect of w'at's a-goin' on in this here drorin'-room ?

Alf.   Never thought of that. (*Amused.*)   I'll slap on the ten bob, and call it seven guineas.

Tom (*bus. ; partly aside*).   An' I gits half, oh !

Alf.   See here !   There are no beds in some of these rooms.

Tom (*as if to start*).   I'll git 'em, sir.

Alf.   Where ?

Tom (*on point of starting*).   Down the street.

   [Alfred *makes a spring, and grabs* Tom *by collar. Tableau.*

Alf. (R. C.).   I say — this sort of thing won't do, you know.   Bring some down from up-stairs.

Tom (L. C.).   Yes, sir. (*Bounds off up* R., *and up stairway* L.)

Alf.   We won't let the rooms up there until these are taken.   Now, let me see — I must roost down here where I can keep an eye on the things.   I'll take this room (R. 2 E.) — it's the smallest of the lot.

Tom (*calling from above*).   Mr. Hastings !   W'ich o' these here beds 'll I fetch down?

Alf.   I'll go and look at them. (*EXIT up* R. *and* L., *and up the stairs.*)

   [*Timid knock several times.   ENTER* Victor Smythe, *door up* R.   *He looks into room cautiously.*

SMYTHE (*near door*).   At last — at last I am here — in
the very house where she lives — under the same roof that
shelters her!   I can scarcely realize it!   It (*hand on heart,
etc., as if its palpitation hurt him*), it is all like a — a dream —
a dream !

> [*Tremendous bang of falling furniture overhead.
> SMYTHE jumps in alarm, and scuds down* R.

TOM (*up-stairs*).   Ge-whiffles !

SMYTHE.   What was that !   (*Hand on heart, etc.*)   Every
noise alarms me, for she said I must be very cautious.   She
must have sent every one out of the way — no one even to
answer the door.   That was so thoughtful of her.   Now, if I
can only get her to consent, and to intercede for me with
Emily, I shall be the happiest man in the whole universe.
And — she has already promised it.   I suppose I ought to let
her know I am here — she — she must be about somewhere.
(*Goes up, and partly off up* R., *looking about.*)   Oh — my heart
seems to almost —

> [*Two large feather beds and blankets fall on* SMYTHE
> *from above, up* R.   SMYTHE *screams out in alarm
> as he falls half buried among them.*   TOM *rushes
> down the stairs and falls to* L. *of* SMYTHE ; *faces
> SMYTHE just as he is rising from among the bed-
> ding, ready to throw bolster.*

TOM (*rising*).   That was odd, now, wasn't it ?

SMYTHE (*rising from under bed*).   Yes — it was a little
odd.   But no matter.

TOM (*glancing critically at the bedding*).   No — there ain't
no pertickler harm done, sir.

SMYTHE.   I knocked several times — but as no one an-
swered, I just looked in.

TOM.   Quite right, sir.   I'll attend to you in just a minute.
(*Rushes up* R., *and drags bedding down across stage toward door
L. 2, upsetting chairs, tables, etc.*)

SMYTHE (*following*).   But I just wanted to see —   (*Steps
on blanket and is tripped by it.   Bus. with tables, etc.*)

Tom (*dragging things*). You can see 'em in a minute, sir. We're just a-puttin' the beds in. (*EXIT* L. 2.)

> [SMYTHE *watches* TOM'S *bus. in astonishment. Hand to heart. Wipes brow, etc.*

SMYTHE. This is one of the servants. What shall I say to him? How — how can I be cautious? And yet she said "be cautious, or you will spoil all."

> [TOM *runs in at door* L. 2.

TOM. Now, sir — ha, ha! (*Bus.*) I suppose you saw it?

SMYTHE (R.; *uncertainly*). Oh, yes.; I — I saw it.

TOM (L.; *to himself*). He saw it! He saw that there bill with "All the Comforts of Home" writ on it. That's w'at fetched 'im.

SMYTHE. I beg your pardon — but I'm afraid I've made a mistake.

TOM (*quickly; alarmed*). Oh, no, you hain't!

> [SMYTHE *startled. Backs up toward door up* R.

Won't you look at the rooms? (*Invitingly.*)

SMYTHE (*uncertainly*). Wh — what rooms?

> [*A bolster falls from above, up* R. SMYTHE, *startled still more, runs down* R.

TOM (*runs quickly up* R., *and calls up stairway*). Say, you don't want to heave down no more o' them fur a minute — I'm a-waitin' on a customer.

SMYTHE (R. C.; *aside*). A — customer! A cus —

TOM (L. C.; *down to* SMYTHE *quickly*). Now, sir, just have a look at 'em. They're simply entrancin'.

SMYTHE. I — I would like to speak to your employer, if you please.

TOM (L. C.). Sorry — but ye can't just now, unless you yell up them stairs. [*READY* ALFRED, *to enter up* R.

SMYTHE (R. C.; *cautiously; mysteriously*). I alluded to the mistress of the house.

TOM. Well, we ain't got as fur as that yet. But the lodgin's —

SMYTHE. How's that! Surely, I have always seen your master in company with a lady.

TOM. Quite likely, sir — an' so have I. But it don't follow as 'e's married to 'er, just from that.

SMYTHE. Not married? Not —

TOM. No, sir — not by no means. But these here lodgin's is —

SMYTHE. Great Heaven! (*Hand to brow, etc.*) Why, this — this is horrible — and I loved the daughter — I — Great Heaven! Where would I have got to had you not opened my eyes? Here! (*Gives* TOM *money.*) Take this! Let me go! (*Starts off door up* R.) Let me go! (*EXIT, door up* R.)

> [*READY knock* R. U. D. TOM, *up at* D. R., *stares after* SMYTHE *an instant. Glances at the money in his hand, then throws the bolster off* R. 3 E., *and meets* ALFRED *as he comes down from above.*

TOM. That there individual ain't had enough sleep lately.

ENTER ALFRED, *coming down stairway up* R.

ALF. (L.; *stopping on stairs as he descends*). Well — have you captured a lodger?

TOM (R.). The man was clean out of his head.

> [ALFRED *and* TOM *advance together.*

ALF. What did he do? (*Comes down and into room.*)

TOM. He inquired for the lady of the house.

ALF. What!   [*READY* DABNEY, *to enter up* R.

TOM. Mebbe it was howin' to them beds fallin' on 'im.

ALF. Great Heavens, Tom! He has escaped us.

TOM. Eh?

ALF. Victor Smythe.

TOM. Ge-whiffles!

> [*Both rush up into room up* L. C. *Throw up window and look out.*

ALF. (*going up* L.). And I promised to receive him!

TOM. I'll go and drag him back, sir! (*Starts* R.)

Alf.   Here!   Stop!   Somebody's just going in at the door!   [*Both look around back to* R. *as if at outside of house-door.*

Tom (*looking out*).   It's the same party, sir.   He's comin' back for somethin'.

Alf.   He'll get it, too.   (*Coming down.*)

Tom (*down with* Alfred *into room*).   That's what he will, sir!

Alf. (*going* R.).   Quick!   Stand by the door here!

Tom.   We won't make no mistake this time.

[Alfred *and* Tom *quickly stand each side of door up* R., *ready to pounce upon* Smythe.   *Knocking on door up* R., *from outside, several times.*   Alfred *and* Tom *signal each other to be ready.*

ENTER Christopher Dabney, *up* R., *quietly and carefully.   He turns to close door, so that his back is toward* Alfred *and* Tom.   Alfred *and* Tom *suddenly jump upon him ferociously.   Both shout or exclaim on climax.*

Alf. *and* Tom.   Now we've got you!   Throttle him! (*Etc.*)   [Dabney *gives cry of terror; they drag him quickly down.*

Alf.   Now, give it to him!   } (*Together.*)
Tom.   Bang his nose for him! }

Tom (*alone; seeing* Dabney).   Stop!   [*Both stop.* This ain't him at all!

Alf. (L. C.).   Oh, the deuce!

[Dabney, C., *gasps and gurgles, overcome with terror.* Beg your pardon, sir — all a mistake!

Tom (R. C.).   Yes — you're the wrong man!   It warn't your fault, though!

Alf. (L. C.).   Very sorry it occurred.

Dabney (C.).   Gi — gi — (*motions*).   A chair!

Alf. *and* Tom.   Yes, sir!   (*They let go of* Dabney.   *He sinks.   They catch him again.   Repeat bus.*   Tom *manages to get chair to him from behind table* R. *They seat him in it with some difficulty,* C. *Bus.*)

DAB. Oh — thank you ! (*Sits* C.)

TOM (R. ; *absent-mindedly*). An' I gits half !

ALF. (L.). It was too bad ; by Jove, it was !

DAB. (C.). Oh — never mind, sir ! I was taken somewhat by surprise — you — the — oh ! The fact is, I am a very nervous man. (*Shakes head sadly.*) Dreadfully nervous. Sometime you shall know why —

ALF. Yes — some other time. (*To* TOM.) A glass of water — quick !

TOM. Yes, sir.

DAB. Sometime — (TOM *brings glass of water from table up stage.*)

ALF. (*taking it*). Have a little water, sir !

            [DABNEY *wobbles nervously in chair.*

TOM. Have another chair !

DAB. Thanks — there on my temples.

         [ALFRED *wets* DABNEY'S *temples with the water.*

TOM (*bus.*). A little on the bald spot, sir ? (*Rubs bald spot on* DABNEY'S *head, and about to pour water from pitcher on his head.*)

DAB. (*bus.*). Don't ! don't ! don't ! (*Bus.*)

            [TOM *stops, alarmed.*

For Heaven's sake, don't rub anything there — friction in that locality sets me all on edge !

TOM. Quite right, sir. (*Goes up* R. *with the pitcher and tumbler, and returns to* R. *of* DABNEY.)

DAB. (*to* ALFRED). I seem to feel better now.

ALF. Very glad, I assure you.

DAB. (*looking at* ALFRED). 'Hem — yes — er. (*Rises.*) Good-morning !

       [TOM *puts back the chair to same place behind table,* R. C.

ALF. How d'ye do ?   [*READY dogs and barking,* L. H.

DAB.   You have — lodgings to let here?

ALF. *and* TOM (*together;* TOM *turning quickly to* DABNEY).
Yes!   Yes, sir!

ALF.   Charming lodgings.

TOM.   Can't be beat.

ALF. (*crosses in front of* DABNEY, *and pushes* TOM *aside.*
TOM *goes round on* DABNEY'S L.).   Will you look at them,
sir?

TOM.   Yes — just take one look, that's all!

> [ALFRED *motions* TOM *to be quiet.*

(L.; *aside.*)   An' I gits half!

DAB. (C.).   Yes — I — give me your arm, please.   I'm
still a little —

ALF. (R.).   Certainly.

TOM.   Cer —

> [*Bus. of* ALFRED *motioning* TOM *off.*   DABNEY *takes*
>   ALFRED'S *arm.*   *They go* L.   TOM *follows eagerly.*

DAB. (*stopping*).   I do hope it's quiet and tranquil here?

ALF.   Perfectly quiet.

TOM.   Peaceful as the tomb, sir.

DAB.   Ugh!   (*Gasp — drawing breath.*)   Don't speak of
such things!

TOM (*quickly starting, as if to prevent another fit*).   No,
sir!   No — I take it back, sir!

DAB.   No — er — children, I hope?

ALF.   Not one.

DAB.   No dogs? cats? parrots? pugs? puppies? cana-
ries, and such things?

TOM.   Anythin' you want, sir, we'll have it cooked to
order!   (*Bus.*)

ALF.   Nothing of the kind, sir!   (*Pulling out paper.*)   You
can see by the rules, sir, how it is.   'Hem.   (*Reads.*)   "First:
rent payable strictly in advance.   Second: children and dogs
must keep off the grass.   Third: anything ordered will be
charged extra."

DAB. Ah — those are the rules ?   Well, I hope they will be enforced about the dogs, anyway.

> [*They go* L.   TOM *opens the door* L. 2.

ALF. Every time, sir !

TOM. If I once ketch a dog here, sir, I'll —

> [DABNEY *goes into room* L. 3.   *Bus. of poodles barking and jumping at his shins — pushed or tossed from outside* L. 3.   DABNEY *yells and jumps about, and falls into chair holding feet in air.*   TOM *and* ALFRED *shout, and bus. of catching poodles, etc.   Keep on for laugh.   Strike picture ;* TOM *holding dogs ;* ALFRED *trying to soothe* DABNEY.

ALF. (*shouting to* TOM).   Take 'em up-stairs !

TOM. Quite right, sir !   (*Rushes off up* R., *and up-stairs with poodles.*)

ALF. (*to* DABNEY).   Don't be alarmed, I beg.

DAB. (*on ottoman*).   Er — er — I can't — bear a dog !

ALF. (L. *of* DABNEY).   Neither can I — they are the most repugnant creatures on the face of the earth to me. The question is, how the devil they came here.   Are they yours ?

DAB. (*rises to* C.).   Mine !   Mercy, no !

> *ENTER* TOM, *up* R.

ALF. (L.).   Thank Heaven for that !   I cannot let lodgings to people who keep dogs !

TOM (R.).   No (*shaking head*), we can't let no one in these here lodgin's as keeps dogs !

ALF. No matter how respectable they otherwise appear.

> [DABNEY *looks helplessly from one to the other, shaking head to signify his innocence.*

But, as you say they are not yours, suppose you just glance at this room — it's much pleasanter than the other.

TOM. Yes.   [*They conduct* DABNEY *down* L. 2.

DAB. (*crosses to* D. L. 2 E.).   Very well, I will look.   But — are you quite sure —

[*They come to door of room* L. 2, *and open it.* DAB-
NEY *bus. of shrinking, and lifting feet, fearing more
dogs.*

ALF.   Oh — quite, sir !   Allow me to look in first —

TOM.   Allow me.   (*Rushes in at* L. 2, *and out again.*)

[ALFRED *takes* C.

Not a vestige of one of 'em, sir — an' the ones as was in
that there room, I dropped 'em off o' the roof o' the house.

DAB. (*sits again on ottoman; bus.; face contortion*).   Er —
oh — oh — don't — don't !

TOM (*getting round behind ottoman to* R. *of* ALFRED).
There he goes again, sir !

ALF. (C., R. *of ottoman*).   What seems to be wrong with
you this time ?

DAB. (*on ottoman*).   Oh — er — the   horrible — idea !
Dropped off the roof !   (*Covers face.*)

TOM.   ALFRED.   OTTOMAN.   DABNEY.

TOM (*to* ALFRED).   It seems to give 'im a fit, sir, which-
ever way you put it.

DAB.   Is this the apartment ?   (*Looks off* L. 2, *while seated
on ottoman.*)

ALF.   Yes — I'm sure it'll please you.

DAB.   Um !   Quiet, you say ?

TOM.   Well, I should say !   The back yard is cat proof,
and we've had the pavin' stones padded, so's to keep 'em
from echoin' when any one whispers.

[*Both looking at him expectantly.*

DAB.   What terms do you ask ?   (*On ottoman.*)

TOM (*by chair* L. *of* R. *table; quickly*).   Er — yes.   What
terms do we ask ?

ALF. (C.).   With breakfast and attendance, six guineas.

TOM (R. ; *aside*).   An' I gits half !   (*Rubs the plush of
chair absent-mindedly* L. *of* R. *table.*)

[DABNEY, *contortion of face.   Shrinking.   Draws up
one leg, etc.*

DAB. (L., *on ottoman; breaking out*). Don't! don't! don't! (*Bus. of facial contortion.*)

TOM (R.). Look out! He's goin' into another o' them spasms.

ALF. (C.) The price is too high?

DAB. (L.; *motioning before he can speak*). Eh! Eh! Eh! For Heaven's sake, don't let him rub that plush — the sound drives me wild!

> [ALFRED *motions* TOM *away.* TOM *retires up a little*
> R. C.

I'll take the lodgings.

TOM (R. C.; *exultantly*). Oh!

DAB. (L.). A month in advance, I believe you said? (*Pays* ALFRED *bills, etc.*)

> [TOM *looks on from up stage, with delight.*

I can move in at once, can't I?

ALF. Certainly. ⎫
TOM. O yes! ⎬ (*Together.*)
⎭

TOM. Sooner, sir, if you like! (*Looks at bills in* AL-FRED'S *hands. Rubs his hands together.*)

> [ALFRED *suddenly clutches* TOM. *Both look at* DAB-
> NEY, *but he does not notice bus.*

ALF. (*to* TOM). If you don't keep away, you'll ruin the whole business!

TOM. Quite right, sir! (*Goes up* R., *to stairs. Starts to bound up stairway, stumbles, and falls on stairs, catching by baluster.*) [DABNEY *and* ALFRED *start in alarm.*

DAB. Oh!

TOM (*quickly on his feet*). An' I gits half! (*EXIT up the stairs,* L.) [*READY knock,* R.

ALF. Calm yourself, sir — he's gone.

> [*READY* LANGHORNE, *to enter up* R.

DAB. That person seems to affect my nerves painfully. I — I was born nervous, sir; an inheritance from my mother. My father was a musician, and I was put through a course to follow the same profession, and soon got an appointment to teach in a large conservatory. That was my ruin. Imagine — imagine — if you can — with my nerves — thirty pianos, innumerable violins, several cornets, piccolos, and cellos,

[ALFRED *sits on arm of chair*, L. *of* R. *table, disgusted.*
crowded together in a rather small building, until the air seemed to split and bellow and boil with a perfect frenzy of the discords of pandemonium. Then, sir, to put a finishing stroke, I was ambitious enough to write an opera — and it was accepted. I quarrelled with the conductor, the soloists, orchestra, chorus-singers, was insulted by the stage-manager, and finally hissed by the audience. (*Rises, and over to* AL-FRED. *Buries face in hands. Last speech very fast.*)

[ALFRED *attempts to rise and get away.* DABNEY *puts him back on arm of chair again.*
Young man, let me advise you, if you want some cheerful occupation for your leisure hours, forge, counterfeit, burglarize, kill, rob, blow up everything with dynamite, commit suicide ; but for Heaven's sake, don't write anything for the theatre !

[DABNEY *crosses in front of* ALFRED *to his* R., *and falls into armchair.* ALFRED *rises from arm, and takes* L.

ALF. No — I've no intention of doing so. (*Aside.*) An interesting case, this is. I'll make my first attempt at practice on him.

[*Knock outside*, R. TOM *rushes down-stairs, and opens door up* R. DABNEY *shrinks on hearing the rush.* ALFRED *soothes him.*

DAB. (*in armchair*). Oh, dear ! What is that rushing and jumping about ?

ALF. (C.). Nothing, sir, I assure you.

[*Bus. of soothing, etc.*
ENTER JUDSON LANGHORNE, *door up* R. *Very much of a swell ; carries a small cane ; red or tan*

gloves; dudish manners, with some impertinence.
Tom *remains up* L.

LANGHORNE (*coming down* L. C.). Aw! Mawning! How de do? Lodgings to let heah?

ALF. (R. C.). Ah — yes.

LANG. (L. C.). Yaas. (*Twirls his cane.*) Ha, ha! I read your bill —

ALF. That's all right, sir — it was put there to read. "All the Comforts of Home."

LANG. (L. C.). Aw, yes — elegantly furnished lodgings — all the comforts of home. Nice ideah — really — ha, ha!

ALF. (C., *to* TOM, *who is up* L.). You attend to the gentleman, Thomas.

TOM. (*down* L. *of* LANGHORNE). Yes, sir. This way, sir! The most excruciatingly elegant apartment as ever you seen in your life lays right here! (TOM *rushes* LANGHORNE *up* L. C.)

LANG. Aw, don't say! Haw, haw!

TOM. Yes, I do say! Haw, haw!

[*EXEUNT* TOM *and* LANGHORNE, *door up* L. C.

DAB. (*seated in armchair*, R.). I hardly like the way that young man flourishes about with his cane. (*Shows nervousness.*)

ALF. Don't believe he'll continue it long, sir. It would exhaust him too much.

DAB. Do you think so?

ENTER LANGHORNE, *followed by* TOM, *up* L.

LANG. (*up at* D. L. C.) I rather like the box, deah boy, and I think I'll take it.

TOM. Quite right, dear boy. (*Goes quickly down* L. *of* ALFRED, *who turns to him, so that* DABNEY *will not hear.*) He's took it, sir!

ALF. Here — you attend to this one. See about his luggage. (*Goes up to* LANGHORNE.)

TOM. Yes, sir. (*Goes to* DABNEY. *Coming suddenly*

at his L. *side, and speaking in his ear.*) Where shall I git it, sir?

ALFRED.   LANGHORNE.
TOM.
TABLE.   DABNEY.

R.   L.

DAB. (*start bus.*). Ugh! (*Contortion of feature bus.*) Don't, don't — don't scream in my ear like that.

TOM (*crosses round behind table, and gets down* R. *of* DABNEY; *to* DABNEY). I was a-askin' about your luggage, sir.

DAB. I'll give you directions, and you must be, oh, so careful! (DABNEY *and* TOM *continue talking in pantomime across the table.*)

TOM.   TABLE.   DABNEY.   .

LANG. (*coming down* L. C., *and kneeling on one knee on ottoman,* L.). Judson Langhorne — yaas, deah boy; ha, ha, ha! I suppose I have the pleasure of addressing the — aw — lord of the — aw — castle. (*Bus., whirl cane, etc.*)

[DABNEY shrinks, and dodges slightly.

ALF. (C.). To some extent, sir. I understand you have decided to take the apartment.

LANG. Yaas — aw — yaas. I'll take it — and I want to go right in, if you don't mind.

ALF. Go in just when you please, sir, and stay in as long as you please. We're free and easy here.

LANG. Aw — free and easy — that suits me chawmingly, deah boy!

LANGHORNE.
TOM.   TABLE.   DABNEY.   ALFRED.   OTTOMAN.

R.   L.

[READY noise L. H.

ALF. But the lodgings, I regret to say, are not free —

[LANGHORNE looks at ALFRED.

although they may be easy.

LANG. (*laughing boisterously*). No — of course not ! Haw, haw !

ALF. And our rule is a month in advance.

LANG. (*sudden drop*). Aw — yaas.

ALF. You grasp the idea, of course ?

LANG. Yaas — I grasp — but — (*bright idea*). Aw — can you change me a fifty-pound note ? (*Hand in pocket.*)

ALF. Oh, yes.

LANG. (*stops, paralyzed*). You can !

ALF. Certainly — send out, and have the change for you in two minutes.

LANG. Aw ! (*Much relieved.*) Aw, no ! Couldn't think of troubling you so much, deah boy. No hurry at all. (*Goes up to door* L. C.) I'll remain right here ; and when you have the change handy, let me know. (*EXIT into room up* L. C., *and closes doors.*)

ALF. Another one ! By Jove, the business is flourishing !

[DABNEY *bus. of gymnastic exercises in explaining things to* TOM. TOM *imitating him, as if trying to get the idea.*

What the deuce is he up to now ?

DAB. Now, don't forget the soda-powders, dumb-bells, rowing-machine, and sponges.

TOM. Quite right, sir.

[LANGHORNE *sings a scale unsuccessfully outside, up* L., *in loud voice. All listen.*

DAB. (*rises ; starts with shriek*). Ah — stop it ! Stop it ! I can't stand it ! (*Bus. of dancing about, but must not overdo it.*)

ALF. Oh, the devil ! (*Goes up to* LANGHORNE'S *door.*)

TOM. Ge-whiffles !

[DABNEY *sits again.* LANGHORNE *begins to sing,* "Down in a Coal Mine."

DAB. Horrors ! What's that he's singing ?

TOM (*up to* ALFRED). "Down in a Coal Mine."

[DABNEY *stops his ears.*

ALF. Hang the coal mine! Go and tell him there's a strike. Stop his howling, someway.

TOM. Yes, sir. I'd do anything in the world for you, sir. (*TOM goes up, and EXIT up* L. C., *closing door. Bus. of singing as he goes. Sudden bus. of stop*, R., *off. Singing stops.*)

DAB. Has — has he stopped? (*Fingers out of ears cautiously.*)

ALF. Yes, sir; it's all right now.

> [*Noise of banging furniture outside, up* L. ALFRED *and* DABNEY *start and turn.*
>
> *ENTER* TOM, *up* L. C., *with bloody face, limping, etc.*

TOM (*down* L. C.; *after the laugh*). Oh, I'd do anything in the world for you, sir!

ALF. (C.). What did the fellow do?

TOM. Ge-whiffles! Can't ye see?

ALF. (*starting toward up* L.). Let me have a word with him.

TOM (*stopping* ALFRED). No, sir! Don't ye do it! I've just had a word with 'im — an' it ain't encouragin'. (*TOM wipes blood from face. He must not fail to remove it.*)

DAB. The fellow is terrible! I shall not stay. (*Starts to go up* C.)

> [ALFRED *and* TOM *both down, remonstrating with* DABNEY. *They bring him down.*

ALF. (L.). But, my dear sir —

TOM (R.). We'll fix 'im for ye. [*READY knock* R.

DAB. (C.). But his singing — (*Contortion of horror.*)

ALF. Stop a moment! An uncle of mine, who also is nervous, had a new thing the other day — an audiphone — just what you want. You put it in your ears, and you can't hear a sound! (*Looks about on table, etc.*)

TOM. Yes, sir; you couldn't hear the last trump ef it was ter be played!

ALF. Here it is. (*Finds a box on desk*, L. *Opens. Hands*

DABNEY *two small articles for the ears.*) There, sir, try it — wonderful!

TOM (R.). Wonderful!

[*READY* FIFI *and* MAID, *to enter up* R.

DAB. (C.). Dear me, I'm so nervous! Is this the way?

[ALFRED L., TOM R.

ALF. *and* TOM. Yes! Yes!

[DABNEY *puts audiphones in his ears, and looks about.*

ALF. (L.). How do you like it?

[DABNEY *looks at* ALFRED *and* TOM, *unconscious of having been addressed.*

TOM (R.). He says, how do you like it?

DAB. (C.). Eh? [ALFRED L., TOM R.

ALF. *and* TOM (*together*). How do you like it?

DAB. (*looks front, delighted*). Ha, ha, ha! I cannot hear a sound!

TOM. You're a broken-down old jackass.

DAB. (*joyfully*). Thanks — a thousand thanks! Perfectly splendid! (*Goes* L.) I won't go. I'll stay. (*Crosses to* L. 2 E.) Ha, ha, ha! (*EXIT*, L. 2 E.)

ALF. By Jove, that was a lucky thought!

TOM. Yes, sir; but we'll want a lot of 'em if that there feller's goin' to keep up his singin' " Down in the Coal Mine."

[*Knock outside, up* R.

ALF. The door, Tom.

TOM. Yes, sir. (*Bounds up* R., *and opens door.*)

ALF. I wonder what kind of a creature we'll get now!

ENTER FIFI ORITANSKI *up* R., *followed by her maid, and ushered in with great ceremony by* TOM, *who backs down near* ALFRED, *and stands admiring her.* FIFI *is dressed very stylishly, but is not over dressed, and has the manner of a lady who knows the world pretty well.* Bus. *of* ALFRED *bowing, etc.* TOM *also bowing in sympathy with* ALFRED, *without knowing it.*

FIFI (R. C.).   You have apartments — furnished — I believe ?

ALF. (L. C.).   Yes, madam.   (*Aside.*)   By Jove, she's
pretty !

TOM (L., *aside*).   Yes, by Jove, she's pretty — ha, ha !
MAID.
FIFI.   ALFRED.   TOM.

ALF. (*to* TOM).   Shut up !

TOM (*starts*).   I said she was —

[Threatening sign from ALFRED.
Quite right, sir.   (TOM *goes up stage rather dejectedly, and
lingers, watching.   To himself absent-mindedly.*)   An' I gits
half !

FIFI (C.).   I am looking for a pretty front room, and a
smaller one adjoining for my maid.

ALF. (*goes to door* L. 3, *and opens it*).   Oh, yes, with maid
adjoining.   Do you think this would suit you at all ?

[FIFI crosses to L., and looks off L. 3.
FIFI.   Oh, charming !   Why, it's the cosiest place I've
seen anywhere.

TOM (R. *of* ALFRED ; *unable to repress himself ; stepping forward*).   Right you are, miss — it's a —

ALF. (L. *of* TOM ; *quickly*, *to* TOM).   Sh ! —   (*Bus.*)

[TOM starts, and retires silenced.
ALF.   Sh ! —

TOM (*aside ; sotto voce*).   Oh, I'd do anything in the world
for you, sir !   [FIFI *has turned, surprised.*

ALF.   Don't be alarmed, miss !   He's harmless.

[TOM gives ALFRED a look.   Turns and goes up R.
FIFI (L., *coming down*).   The apartment is lovely.   But
this room — whose is this ?

ALF. (*down* C.).   This is a drawing-room which is for the
use of all.   We thought it would be a pleasant innovation.

TOM (*up* R.).   All the comforts o' —

[Bus.   ALFRED stops TOM.

FIFI (L.). Oh, what a charming idea! But I'm afraid such apartments will be far too expensive for me.

ALF. (C.). 'Hem! [TOM *comes down a little, listening.* Oh, no — only — six guineas.

FIFI. Oh!

ALF. Er — five pounds.

TOM (*down to* ALFRED, R., *quickly*). No, sir! No, sir! It was six quid, sir. Six quid! (*Bus. Alarmed.*)

ALF. (C., *shaking* TOM *off*). Hold your tongue!

TOM (R. C., *aside; sotto voce; sadly*). An' I gits half!

FIFI (L.). My, that isn't high at all!

TOM (*aside*). No, it ain't!

FIFI. I will take the rooms, if you please.

ALF. (*bowing*). Delighted, I assure you.

FIFI. There's my card. (*Takes out pretty case. Hands* ALFRED *card. Turns and looks off* L. *again.*)

ALF. Ah! Thank you. (*Absently fondles card to breast.*) I — I — 'hem —

FIFI (*turning*). Well?

ALF. Yes — that is — I hope you will like it here.

FIFI (*graciously*). Ah — how could I help it — such a sweet place — and such a charming landlord!

ALF. *and* TOM (*together*). Ah!

TOM (*aside, exultantly*). An' I gits half!

FIFI (*to maid*). Gretchen, have my things brought over here. [*READY knock* R.

GRETCHEN (*up* R.). Yes'm. (*EXIT*, R. U. D.)

[*READY* BENDER, JOSEPHINE, *and* EVANGELINE, *to enter up* R.

FIFI. I suppose I can move right in?

ALF. *and* TOM (*together*). Oh, yes!

FIFI. You see, if I went, you might forget and rent the rooms to somebody else. (*Laughs, and EXIT at* L. 3.)

[ALFRED L. C., TOM R. C.

ALF. *and* TOM (*eagerly*). Oh, no! (ALFRED *and* TOM *recover, and look at each other.*)

ALF. (*breaking and coming forward a little*, L.).   By Jove,
she's a beauty !   Such an air of aristocracy !   Wonder what
her name — oh !   (*Looks at card.*)   " Fifi Oritanski ! "
Charming name !

TOM (R.).   Ain't it divine !

ALF.   An angel — such grace — and her eyes — did you
notice her eyes, Tom ?

TOM.   I noticed one on 'em, sir.

ALF. (L. C.).   One of them !   What do you mean ?

TOM (R. C.).   It was all as I had a call on — seein as I
gits half.

ALF.   Oh — ha, ha — I forgot that !   And, by the way
(*takes out bills and offers* TOM *part of them*), here's your share
of what I got from the old duffer in there.

TOM (*stoutly*).   No, sir !

ALF.   It's your share, I say.

TOM.   No, sir !   (*Shakes head.*)   I wouldn't take it on no
account.   It ain't the money I cares for — it's only the bare
idea of gittin' half.   No, sir !

ALF.   Oh, well, I'll settle with you some other time.
Come, we must finish up-stairs.   (ALFRED *and* TOM *start
up* R., *quickly.*)   We may let apartments up there yet.

          [*EXEUNT* ALFRED *and* TOM *up-stairs, up* R.

TOM (*as they go*).   Quite right, sir !

          [*Pause.   Knock on door up* R. *several times.*
          ENTER, door up R., THEODORE BENDER, JOSEPHINE
          BENDER, *and* EVANGELINE BENDER.   *They look
          about for some one as they come in.*

BENDER.   This is the place, I suppose.

JOSEPHINE.   Why didn't you ring the bell ?

BEND.   I couldn't find any bell.

EVANGELINE (*timidly*).   Papa, wasn't the bill on the house
next to this ?   [*They come down into room.*

BEND.   No, no !

JOS. (*coming down* R. ;   *sinking into chair* R. *of* R.

table). Theodore, it's outrageous! I cannot walk another step. [*READY* DABNEY, *to enter* L. 2 E.

BEND. (*coming down* C.). Whose fault is it, I'd like to
know? You are never suited. I have said from the first
we ought to have spent our few weeks in town at a hotel.
There is one at the next corner. (*Sits* L. *of* R. *table.*)

[EVANGELINE *surveying the room* C., *demurely.*

JOS. That will do, Theodore. I know perfectly well why
you prefer a hotel. [EVANGELINE *sits back of table.*
I've noticed how you — Evangeline, you needn't cock up
your ears when your father and mother are discussing family
affairs. [EVANGELINE *rises and examines pictures which hang
on wall at* R.

I've noticed that you were much more interested in the
attractiveness of the waiting-maids than in the comfort of
the room.

BEND. Oh, Josephine, my dear!

JOS. In addition to that, the expenses are simply scandalous.

BEND. Well, well, we need not mind a few pounds more
or less. We've feathered our nest pretty well.

JOS. Yes; because I keep my thumb on your hardly earned
shillings — and I intend to do so still.

BEND. (*sighs*). I know it.

JOS. Is there a living soul in this house?

BEND. (*rises and crosses to* L.). Ah, here's some one at last!
ENTER DABNEY *from his room at* L. 2. *Goes up*
C., *delighted, not observing the* BENDERS, *and down*
to C.

DAB. (C., *walking up and down in great glee*). An excel-
lent invention! I can hear absolutely nothing! (*Comes* C.)

JOS. (R. C.; *meeting* DABNEY, C.). Sir, we have come to
look at the —

[DABNEY *stops and looks at her.* *READY* TOM *and*
ALFRED, *to enter up* R.

BEND. (L., *coming on L. of* DABNEY). We want to see the apartment, sir. [DABNEY *looks blank,* C.

Jos. (R. C.). Why, he must be hard of hearing!

[BENDER L., JOSEPHINE R. C., EVANGELINE R.

BEND.
Jos. } (*together ; coming close to* DABNEY; *loud voice*).
EVAN. } We want to look at the rooms.

DAB. (C.). Did somebody make a remark?

EVANGELINE. JOSEPHINE. DABNEY. BENDER.
R.   L.

[*READY* LANGHORNE *and* FIFI *to sing outside* L. *Cello crash* L. 2 E.

Jos. (*gesturing, etc.*). Rooms! Rooms! Rooms! (*Etc.*)

[BENDER *joins in the effort. Motions* EVANGELINE. *She joins also in a sweet, high key.*

EVANGELINE R.   JOSEPHINE R. C.   BENDER L.

Jos.
BEND. } (*together*). Rooms! Rooms! Rooms! (*They*
EVAN. } *stop, out of breath.*)

DAB. (C.; *after looking at them an instant*). Delightful! Heavenly! Ha, ha! (*Dances a little.*)

[JOSEPHINE, EVANGELINE, *and* BENDER *move away each side, alarmed.*

EVAN. Mamma, what's the matter with him?

Jos. He's crazy — don't go near him, child. Come! Come! [JOSEPHINE *and* EVANGELINE *move up stage in alarm. ENTER* TOM *and* ALFRED, *rushing down-stairs, up* R.

ALF. For Heaven's sake, get him away; he'll ruin the whole business!

TOM. Quite right, sir! (TOM *darts across to* L., *and hustles* DABNEY *off into his room at* L. 2, *going in with him.*)

[ALFRED *down, and bowing, etc., to the* BENDER *family, as if nothing were wrong.*

ALF. (C.). It was all a mistake, madam, I assure you.

I am the proprietor of the house.   [*READY crash off*
            L. 2 E.

EVANGELINE R.   JOSEPHINE R. C.   BENDER L. C.

JOS.
EVAN. } *(together)*. Oh !
BEND.

        [*READY* TOM *and* DABNEY, *to enter* L. 2 E.

ALF. (C.). That was merely a nervous gentleman who is quite deaf.

BEND. Yes — we noticed it.

ALF. *(aside)*. By Jove ! What a lovely girl !

JOS. Hum ! We came to look at the lodgings, sir, which you advertise.

ALF. Ah ! Yes? *(Expectantly.)*

JOS. But I'm afraid you haven't very quiet people here.

ALF. Let me assure you, madam, they are so quiet that it is like a Sunday-school.

        [JUDSON LANGHORNE *suddenly sings outside, up* L. C.,
        " Home, Sweet Home," *in loud voice. All start.*

JOS. Mercy ! What is that dreadful noise?

ALF. *(aside)*. Confound the fellow — he will make a beggar of me !

        [FIFI *suddenly starts in, outside* L. 3, *practising the
        scales.*
        *MUSIC. — Lively music pp. ; continue to the end of
        Act, growing louder for bus. near end.*

BEND. *(pricking up his ears)*. Ah ! A woman's voice ! *(Starts toward* L. 3.)

JOS. Theodore !

        [BENDER *stops suddenly. Noise of banging and
        crashing outside* L. 2 E. *All start, and look about
        alarmed.*
            ENTER TOM, *rushing on from* L. 2.

TOM *(calls)*. Help ! Help !

        [*Outside* L. 2, *just before his entrance.*

Help! Oh, Mr. Hastings! The man in there has got them audiphones down in his ears, an' he can't git 'em out! He's smashin' everythin' to smithereens! [*READY curtain.*

NOTE. — *Keep music and all noises down, so that this speech will not fail to be heard, as it is very important. Noise of banging furniture and crashing glass outside* L. 2. *All start, alarmed. Bus.*

> *ENTER* DABNEY, *rushing on* L. 2, *in agony, dancing about, overturning furniture, and calling for help at the top of his voice.* JOSEPHINE *and* EVANGELINE *scream, and run hither and thither to* R. *of* R. *table.* BENDER *dodges, alarmed, also calling out.* TOM *and* ALFRED *hold* DABNEY *by his coat, but the garment is torn and ripped.*

DAB. Help! Pull 'em out! Help! It'll be the death of me! [*RING curtain.*

EVANGELINE.	TABLE.	BENDER	ALFRED	DABNEY	TOM
JOSEPHINE.	in chair.	holding Dabney's coat-tail.	kneeling, back to audience.	on ottoman, holding the other tail of Dabney's coat.	

CURTAIN.

ACT II.

SCENE. — Same as Act I. Some small changes should be made in position of furniture, etc., merely as if a few days had passed, and the house had been used. READY LANGHORNE *and* TOM *to enter up* R.

> *MUSIC. — Lively comedy music to take curtain up. Stop on entrance of* LANGHORNE.

> *ENTER* JUDSON LANGHORNE, *door up* R., *from outside, in haste, as if he had been pursued by some one. He closes door with bang, and stands a moment, breathing hard. Soon he strolls down into room, recovering himself.*

LANGHORNE. What a dooce of a chase the fellow gave me ! (*Wipes brow carefully. Twirls mustache.*) Upon my soul, I had no ideah my tailor could run so. He ought to enter for one of the — aw — what do you call — it's at the Agricultural Hall. Lucky thing I threw him off the scent ; for if he found out I'm heah— dooce take it — I'd have to move again.

> *ENTER* TOM, *door up* R., *with tray of breakfast things.*

Look heah !

TOM (*who was crossing with tray, stops suddenly*). Same to you, sir.

LANG. (L. C.). In case any one should honor me with a call during the course of the next few days — I'm — aw — not at home. (*Turns, and goes up to his door.*)

> [*READY bells up* R. *and* L. 2 E., *and also the* VOICE.

(*Turning.*) You'd better remember it too, or I'll cut off your ears.

Tom (R.). Quite right, sir; and when you undertake it, you'll find as the ears has got somethin' to say on the subject. [*READY* ALFRED, *to enter* R. 2 E.

LANG. (*bullying*). What—you dare to — (*as if to strike with cane*). [Tom *threateningly draws back the breakfast-tray.*

Tom (R.). Look out, or you'll git a dose of coffee an' eggs what'll refresh ye wonderful! You took me by surprise the other day, when ye flung that there furnitoor about; but ye better lay low now, ef ye know what's good for ye.

LANG. (L.). Such—aw—impertinence—from a servant!

Tom (R.). I'd respectfully inform you as I ain't no servant. No, sir! (*Swelling up with dignity.*) I'm in on it.

LANG. In on it?

Tom (*turning grandly*). Yes — in on it. (*Proudly.*) I gits 'alf. [*EXIT* LANGHORNE *into his room up* L. C. *Bell rings violently in* DABNEY'S *room, outside* L. 2.

(Tom *suddenly drops from his grand manner.*) Comin', sir — comin'! (*Starts down towards* L. 2.)

[*Bell rings from upstairs, up* R.

(Tom *stops — starts up* R.) There goes that up-stairs lodger, as always wants to know what time it is. (*Calls up-stairs.*) Well, sir!

VOICE (*above, up* R.). Won't somebody tell me what time it is? [*Bell rings violently in* DABNEY'S *room,* L. 2.

Tom (*starts down* L. 2). It's a quarter before — (*Breaks and starts* L.) Comin', sir — comin'!

[*Bell up-stairs, as before.*

VOICE (*above*). I say, can't somebody tell me what time it is?

Tom. Be there in a minit, sir. (*Starts to* D. L. 2.)

VOICE. Twenty minutes to what?

ENTER ALFRED, *from door* R. 2.

ALF. Tom, hold on ! (*To* C.)

[*READY bell again up* R. *and* L. 2. TOM *stops and meets* ALFERD *near* C.

Has she been out ?   [TOM *looks blankly at* ALFRED. (ALFRED *glances* R.) Have you — have you seen her this morning ?

TOM (L. C.). No, sir, I ain't. Who did you mean ?

ALF. (R. C.). Why — the little — er (*motions* R.) — that is — Miss Bender.

TOM. Oh, yes, sir ; I seen her.

ALF. (*eagerly*). Yes ; did she — did she leave any word — any —

TOM. Oh, yes ; I'd almost forgot — I —

[*Bell rings violently in* DABNEY'S *room, outside* L. 2. Oh, Lord ! Yes, sir ! Coming ! (TOM *starts* L. 2.)

ALF. But wait — I want to know — wait !

[TOM *stops. Bell rings up-stairs, up* R.

VOICE (*outside, up* R., *above*). Is anybody going to tell me what time it is, or not ?

[TOM *starts up a little. Bell rings violently in* DAB-NEY'S *room,* L. 2. *READY bell again,* L.

TOM. Ge-Whiffles ! Could you just tell that up-stairs man the time ? If I don't give the musical galoot this here breakfast, he'll have one of them terrible spasms. (TOM *rushes off at* L. 2, *with tray*.)

ALF. (C., *going up*). Confound the up-stairs man ! He's the worst nuisance in the lot. (*Calls up-stairs, up* R.) Did anybody speak up there ?

VOICE (*up-stairs*). Yes, I spoke — Struthers.

ALF. Ah, I thought I heard your voice, Mr. Struthers. Did you want anything ?

VOICE (*up-stairs*). Want anything ? My soul ! I've been asking what time it is, at the top of my voice, for the past fifteen minutes. I want to set my watch.

ALF. Sorry you had so much trouble. It is now between a quarter-past ten and twenty minutes before two. (ALFRED *comes forward with an air of triumph.*)

VOICE (*up-stairs, very distinctly*). Thanks. I was five minutes slow.

ALF. (*aside*). Well, by Jove! (*Comes down, looking longingly at door* R. 3.) It's useless. I can't do anything but watch for her — and think of her — and dream of her. The sweet little witch, with her roguish eyes! How shy she was at first; but when her charming timidity wore away — when she grew to have confidence in me — (*An ecstactic look; he sinks on chair. Sighs. Suddenly looks up.*) Great Heavens! What have I been thinking of all this time! (*Rises.*) Oh, this is outrageous! I didn't suppose the little darling would take everything I said in earnest, until I found I was taking it in earnest myself. I must pull up, confound me! I must let her know in some way of my engagement to Emily.

              ENTER TOM L. 2., *hurrying on.*

TOM (C.). Say, since you've been a-doctorin' that cove in there, he's took on most singular.

ALF. (R., *seated*). I'll look in on him again, by and by.

TOM. Ef I was you, I wouldn't. Every time you look in he takes on worse.   [*Bell rings in* DABNEY'S *room,* L. 2. Yes, sir! Coming! (TOM *starts* L.) He'll git that bell wore out ef he goes on like this. (*Stops suddenly.*) Ge-Whiffles! (*Takes out note from pocket.*) I'd nearly forgot it again, sir. She told me to give it into your own hands, and I —

              [*READY* BENDER, *to enter* R. 3 E.

ALF. (R., *snatches note*). What! (*Opens eagerly.*)

TOM (*aside*). There's one thing sure, an' that is that he's took clean off his feet.

           [*Bell rings in* DABNEY'S *room, outside* L. 2. Coming, sir — coming! (*Exit* L.)

ALF. (*absorbed in note — reads*). "Dear Mr. Hastings: Mamma and papa are going out this morning, but I have such a dreadful headache that I cannot go with them. I hope you will not be alarmed about the headache, as it is one of the kind that comes on when I would rather have a call from some one I know than go to the Park." (ALFRED *laughs ecstatically, and kisses the note.*) "I have so much to tell you, and I hope you will be glad to see me. Your own Evangeline." (ALFRED *looks up ecstatically.*) "Your own Evangeline !" (*Kisses note again. Sudden revulsion. Starts to his feet.*) By Jove ! Gone as far as this already ! (*Walks about.*) Oh, see here, my boy, this sort of thing won't do ! It won't do at all. (*Rises and crosses to* D. *up* L.)

> *ENTER* BENDER R. 3, *carrying pipe and bag of to-*
> *bacco, etc. He looks at* ALFRED *a moment, holding*
> *door open behind him.*

JOSEPHINE (*speaks outside* R. 3). Now, remember what I say !

BENDER (*speaking back through* R. 3). Yes, my love. (*Closes door quickly, with muttered blasphemy. Turns.*)

> [ALFRED *and* BENDER *facing each other.*

Young man, I am about to give you a piece of advice.

ALF. (L. C. ; *smiles*). Kind, I'm sure !

BEND. (R. C.). Before you marry, ask your intended her opinion of the fragrant weed. She will tell you at that time that she adores it. Proceed at once to write this statement down in black and white, and make her sign it.

ALF. (*laughing*). Is that a necessary formality

BEND. It'll save you many unhappy hours. (*Glances nervously,* R.) You may now witness the result of my failure to procure such a document. (*Holds up pipe, etc.*) I am driven from home. Dressing gown and slippers must be abandoned in order to find a place outside for a soothing whiff.

ALF. Not outside. Right here, Mr. Bender.

BEND. (*pleased*). You allow it ?

ALF. Certainly. "All the Comforts of Home," you know.

BEND. Yes; but that isn't a comfort (*bus.*) — of home (*bus.*) — according to my experience — ha, ha! (BENDER *lights pipe with great satisfaction. Chuckles. Bus. Smokes.*) I'd like to compliment you, Mr. Hastings.

ALF. How so?

BEND. You've got a way with you, sir, that affects my wife in a most extraordinary manner. (*Puffing.*)

ALF. You surprise me!

BEND. Really! Makes her almost amiable. (BENDER *starts suddenly, and looks at door* R. 3.)

> [*READY*, bell up R.

ALF. (*laughing*). Oh, I'm sure she is always that.

BEND. (*dryly*). Are you? (*Puffs.*)

JOS. (*opening door*, R. 3). Theodore!

BEND. Yes, my angel! What did you wish?

JOS. Oh, I only want to keep track of you, that's all. (*Closes door*, R. 3.)

> [BENDER *motionless. Face impassive. Exchanges a*
> *glance with* ALFRED. ALFRED *amused.* *READY*
> TOM *to enter*, L. 2 E.

BEND. (*after above bus.*). That's all. Possibly you think it's a pleasure to be under police supervision.

ALF. (*laughingly*). But I'm afraid you give Mrs. Bender some reason for this distrust.

> [BENDER *pleased. Takes pipe out of mouth. Eyes*
> *twinkle. He glances around.*

BEND. Well, I must confess that I have always been — 'hem — an admirer — a devoted admirer — of the fair sex. (*Rises and walks nearer to* ALFRED.) And I cannot say entirely without success. Ha, ha, ha! (*Laughs, and digs* ALFRED *in the ribs.*) [*Both laugh.*

ALF. Ha, ha! I begin to see.

BEND. Of course in our little town there isn't much latitude.

ALF. No; rather limited, I suppose.

BEND.   Yes, decidedly.   (*Glances* R.)   Decidedly limited. But here in London I did hope to have a little romance or two.

ALF.   And Mrs. B., I presume, is keeping the latitude down pretty low here?

BEND.   Down to nothing, sir.   [*ENTER* TOM, L. 2.

TOM (*crossing up to* R.).   Now he's a-callin' fur camomile tea and a bottle of chloroform.   (*Just going out, up* R.)

[*Bell rings up-stairs, up* R. (*From door. Shouting up-stairs.*) Quarter-past eleving! (TOM *rushes off door up* R.)

BEND. (R. C.).   I say, what female voice did I hear a short time ago?

ALF. (L. C.).   Oh, that was Miss Oritanski.

[*READY* FIFI *to enter*, L. 3 E.

BEND.   Ah— er! Miss Oritanski lives in the house, then?

ALF.   Oh, yes; her apartments are there — opposite yours. (*Amused at* BENDER's *eager interest.*)

BEND.   Indeed! Such charming neighbors — and I didn't know it! I — ha, ha! (*Looks longingly at* L. 3.)

JOS. (*coming to door* R. 3).   Theodore, are you there?

BEND. (*starts visibly*).   Eh — oh — yes, yes; I'm here! (*Grinds his teeth and mutters.*)

[JOSEPHINE *closes door*, R. 3 E.   *ENTER* TOM, *door up* R.

TOM (*to* C.).   Doctor, that there nervous galoot ordered a drink o' chloroform, an' them drug-shop chaps won't let me have it unless I gits an order.

ALF. (L. C.).   I'll go and write you a prescription — one that 'll make him sleep for a month.

TOM.   Yes, sir. Wish you would, sir.

ALF.   Make yourself perfectly comfortable, Mr. Bender. (*Crosses to* R. 2 E.   *EXIT* R. 2 E., *followed by* TOM.)

BEND. (*following a little way up* R.).   Thanks, my boy. I'm perfectly comfortable (*turning front*), so long as Mrs. Bender doesn't come out.   [*Door* L. 3 *opens.*

Ah, I really believe — Miss Oritanski is — ha, ha ! (*Glances nervously* R. 3, *etc.*)   *ENTER* FIFI, L. 3. Upon my soul, she's pretty as a picture ! (*Chuckles. Delighted and anxious bus.*)

FIFI (*down* L.; *aside*). Dear me, what can I do ? My dressmaker will not send the other costume unless I pay her bill to-day, and the management has refused to advance me another penny. (*Sits in front, and on ottoman* L. C.)

BEND. (*aside*). Wonder if I could venture to address her ? (*Glances around toward his wife's door,* R. 3.) I'll chance it, anyhow. (*Takes a hasty survey of himself in a large mirror up* R. *Bus. of arranging tie or something. He comes down, with a slight embarrassment, and a trifle of anxiety as to door* R. 3.) Ah — ha — ha — Miss Oritanski, I believe !

[FIFI *looks quickly around at* BENDER. I hope you won't take offence at my seeming presumption, but as I'm to some extent a neighbor of yours, I thought you might allow me to introduce myself.

FIFI (L. C.). Certainly — what name ?

BEND. (R.). E — Bender — Theodore — Theodore Bender. And entirely and most devotedly at your service.

FIFI (*politely, but with a slight frigidity*). Very much pleased, I'm sure.

BEND. (*approaching her ; gives a glance toward door,* R. 3.). I — 'hem — I am a retired — e — business man — from one of the provincial towns, and am spending a few weeks in London for pleasure, and — e — recreation — recreation. (*Smiles, etc. Bus. of glancing at door,* R. 3.)

FIFI (*aside; the dawn of a sudden idea shown by her eyes*). Retired ! Then he's rich. (*Rises to* L., *and bows. Aloud.*) You cannot imagine how pleased I am at having such an agreeable neighbor. (*Sits again.*)

BEND. (*aside; chuckles*). She likes me ! (BENDER *lingers near* R., *occasionally looking nervously at his wife's door.*)

[FIFI *near* L. Are you here — for — e — recreation ?

FIFI. Oh, dear, no! I'm not so fortunate as that. I have an engagement.

BEND. (C.; *not understanding*). Oh — engagement?

FIFI (*on ottoman*). Yes. I am singing at the Opera Comique.

BEND. Opera Comique! [FIFI *nods demurely*.
(*Aside.*) An actress! (*Chuckles.*) The dream of my life has been to meet one, and here it is actually fulfilled. The dream of my life fulfilled — and (*sudden change*) — the dream of my wife in the next room.

FIFI. Won't you sit down, Mr. Bender.

BEND. Ah, thank you. (*He is about to accept the invitation, and starts toward* FIFI *as if to sit. He stops suddenly, and looks nervously at his wife's door,* R. 3.) Ahem — I — I believe I'd rather stand. (*With a longing look at the seat by* FIFI'S *side.*) My doctor has ordered me to — e — take all the exercise I can.

FIFI. And won't he let you sit down? Dear me! How dreadfully you must suffer.

BEND. Yes — I suffer (*glances* R.) — more than I can tell. (*Aside.*) Oh! if we were only somewhere else! (*A thought.*) I wonder if I could? (*Goes to door,* R. 3. *Pause.*) I'll try it. Confound it, I'd try anything. (*He quietly turns key in door. Look of joy.*) Ha, ha! (*Chuckles.*) I've locked her in!

FIFI. Mr. Bender!

BEND. (*starts*). Eh — oh, yes! (*Goes toward* FIFI *with great relief evident in his manner.*) I was just — e — locking my door.

FIFI. I saw you were.

BEND. So many valuables in there — it's safer, you know.

FIFI. Yes. (*Nodding demurely.*) Safer to keep them there.

BEND. Yes, ha, ha! (*Laughs in an uncertain manner.*)
[FIFI *bursts into a merry laugh.*

(BENDER *laughs with her; then suddenly stops.*) 'Hem — e — perhaps we'd better not laugh quite so audibly.

FIFI. Perhaps not — the valuables might hear.

BEND. Ahem — yes, they might. (BENDER *about to sit by* FIFI'S *side,* L. C., *on ottoman.*)

FIFI (*rises*). What! disobeying the doctor's orders, Mr. Bender? (*Sits.*)

BEND. Oh — d — e — hang the doctor's orders! (*Sits* R., *on ottoman.*) Er — Miss Oritanski — I've been smoking here. If I'd known you were coming out —

FIFI. Don't speak of it, Mr. Bender. I like it.

BEND. (*rapturously; aside*). She likes it. (*Aloud.*) So you're singing at the Opera Comique? [FIFI *nods assent.* What — e — what part?

FIFI. In the new piece to-morrow, I'm Prince Vladimir.

BEND. Prince Vladimir! (*Draws a sigh of delight.*) How perfectly — e — sweet you must look in the part of a prince.

FIFI. I'm going to try one of the costumes on this morning. Would you like to see it?

BEND. Like to — I — (*Sudden stop, and look at door* R 3.)
               [FIFI *laughs lightly, amused.*
It would delight me beyond words.

FIFI. There's only one obstacle.

BEND. (*bus. of looking* R.). I know it.

FIFI (*laughingly*). Oh, I don't mean the valuables.

BEND. What, another!

FIFI. Ah, Mr. Bender! I am afraid you don't know dressmakers.

BEND. Well, I've met — 'hem — a few.

FIFI. But not mine. Oh, she's a tyrant! Now, what do you think she has done to-day?

BEND. (*blinking in expectation of a horrible revelation*). What has she done to-day?

FIFI. Refused to send my most important costume because there is a trifle due on the bill. Of course I shall send to the management and have it attended to, but the delay — and the insult! (*Rises to* R. *Walks indignantly.*) The humiliation!

BEND. (*rises and follows to* C.). Outrageous! (*Thinks.*) My dear young lady — would you consider it intrusive (*rises*) — if I — if — I asked the favor of — e — arranging this little matter?

FIFI (R. ; *turning; feigned surprise*). You!

BEND. (C.). Ah — don't misconstrue me! It has been the dream of my life — to — e — do something for Art.

FIFI. Oh, how good you are! I feel that you are a friend. (*Impulsively holds out her hands.*)

> [BENDER *eagerly kisses her hand;* FIFI *retreats quickly a step or two.* BENDER *bus. of glance* R. 3, *and of uncertain smile at* FIFI, *etc.*

Ah, I am afraid I have been too frank with you!

BEND. No, no, not at all! Not at all!

FIFI. And yet — it seems to me that I could trust you.

BEND. You could — you could!

FIFI (*crosses to* L.). But (*speaks doubtfully*) I'm dreadfully afraid it would hardly be right.

BEND. Yes, but —

FIFI. Well, I will put your friendship to the test. Wait just a moment, and I'll get the bill. (*EXIT quickly*, L. 3.)

> [*READY* JOSEPHINE, *to enter* R. 3 E.

BEND. (*delighted; chuckles; bus.*) Ha, ha! We're getting along charmingly. Charmingly! Ah (*walking*), I haven't forgotten all I knew. No! (*Shaking head in merriment, etc., and chuckling to himself. Comes before his wife's door* R. 3, *and stops; stands looking at it.*) And Josephine locked in too, ha, ha, ha! That wasn't bad, now — that wasn't half bad!

> *ENTER* FIFI, L. 3, *with a bill.*

FIFI (L.). Here it is, Mr. Bender.

BEND. (C.). Give it to me.

FIFI (*playfully holding it away*).   My, how imperious you are!   (*Imitates him.*)   "Give it to me."

BEND.   Ah — but I beg — (*Tries to get the bill.*)

FIFI (*bus.*).   You are in a hurry because you want to get rid of me.   [JOSEPHINE *tries to open door* R. 3.

JOS. (*rattling door; outside* R. 3).   Theodore! Theodore!

BEND.   Here, quick! Yes, my love!

FIFI.   There, take it! (*Hurriedly puts bill into* BENDER'S *hand.   Skips to door* L. 3.)   Ta-ta!   (*Throws a kiss to* BENDER, *and EXIT* L. 3.)

JOS. (*outside* R. 3).   Theodore! what does this mean?

BEND. (*hastening to door* R. 3).   What is it, my angel?

JOS. (*outside* R. 3).   Open this door.

BEND.   Why, is it locked?   (*Unlocks and opens door.*) How did that occur?

> *ENTER* JOSEPHINE, R. 3, *dressed for the street, and bringing* BENDER'S *hat and cane.   Putting them on table* R., *and coming down* C.   *She strides on, looking about in silence, and with evident suspicion.*

JOS. (R. C.).   Did you lock that door?

BEND. (*down* L. C.).   I, my love!

JOS.   It's perfectly evident that you did.

BEND. (*looking at his pipe*).   Ah — ahem — you — I was smoking — and —

JOS.   Well?

BEND.   I thought the smoke might get in, you know. Ahem — (*Slight start, realizing he has made a blunder.*)   Of course it must have been in a fit of abstraction, my dear.

JOS.   Um!   It was a fit of something, I've no doubt. (*Aside.*)   I wonder if anything has been going on?

> [*READY* TOM *and* ALFRED *to enter up* R. *and* R. 2 E., *respectively.*

BEND. (*aside*).   She'll be over it before long. (BEN-DER *glances aside at the bill.   Starts.*)   Ha, eighty-six pounds!

JOS. (*crosses to* L.; *turning*). I am ready to go now, The-odore.

BEND. (*crosses down* R.; *aside*). Jerusalem! I haven't a fiver to my name. She takes care of the money. Now, how the devil —

JOS. (*down* C.). What is the matter with you this morning?

BEND. Eh? Me? Oh — nothing. Come, my dear. (*Starts up* R.)

JOS. (*following; aside*). I shall watch that man very closely.

BEND. (*up* R.). Isn't Evangeline coming?

JOS. You know very well she has a headache.

BEND. I thought it might be better.

JOS. (*buttoning glove*). She says it's worse — and —. (*Aside.*) Now, I think of it, I'd better just lock the door. One can never be too careful with young girls. (*Bus. of locking door* R. 3, *and putting key into her pocket.*)

BEND. (*up* R.). Good Lord, I've got to get this money somehow!

JOS. (*going up* R. *to table, to get hat and cane*). There's your hat. There's your cane. (*She jams his hat upon his head.*) Come!

BEND. Yes, my angel! (*Turns at door up* R., *and glances toward* FIFI'S *door.*)

> *ENTER* TOM *up* R., *and* ALFRED R. 2 E., *meeting* JOSEPHINE *and* BENDER. TOM *has a cup of tea and a package; he crosses toward* L. 2. *EXIT* L. 2.

JOS. (*up* C.; *sweetly*). Ah, Mr. Hastings, good-morning!

> [ALFRED *bows politely.*

ALF. (*crosses around in front of table, and up to* L. *of* JOSE-PHINE). Good-morning, my dear Mrs. Bender. Off for a little constitutional?

JOS. (*very pleasantly*). Yes; isn't it a lovely day? (*Very sweetly.*) Come, Theodore!

> [BENDER *gets in a look at* ALFRED. *Eyes up.*

ALF. A very charming time to you!

BEND. (*to* ALFRED, *at door*). Oh, don't, my boy!

[*READY bell and voice, up* R. JOSEPHINE *laughs.*
EXEUNT BENDER *and* JOSEPHINE, *up* R.

ALF. (*coming down*). They're safely gone. Now to Evangeline! (*Goes to door* R. 3, *and knocks cautiously.*) The little darling!

[*READY* LANGHORNE *and* EVANGELINE, *to enter*
L. C. *and* R. 3 E., *respectively.*

EVAN. (*outside* R. 3). Who is it?

ALF. How is your headache, Miss Bender?

EVAN. (*outside* R. 3). Oh, is it you? (*Tries to open door.*)

ALF. Yes; who else should it be?

EVAN. Why, I can't get out.

ALF. Is the door locked?

EVAN. (*outside* R. 3). Yes; isn't the key there?

ALF. No; but I'll soon have one. (*Feels quickly in pockets. Glances about. Runs to table and looks.*)

ENTER TOM *from* L. 2.

TOM (*going across quickly toward up* R.). Now he wants a mustard plaster, and a pail o' hot water for his feet.

ALF. Tom!

TOM (*startled*). Ge Whiffles! I didn't see you, sir.

ALF. Haven't you any keys about you? I must open that door.

TOM (*pulling out bunch of keys*). Quite right, sir. (*Tosses them to* ALFRED.) I ain't never seen nothin' that one o' them wouldn't open. (*Hurries to door up* R.)

ALF. Ah — thanks.

TOM. Don't mention it. (*Aside.*) An' I gits 'alf! (*Starts off.*)   [*Bell rings overhead, up-stairs, at up* R.
(*Yelling up-stairs*). 'Alf-past eleving!   [*EXIT, door up* R.

VOICE (*above, up-stairs up* R.). I want to know what — oh —

ENTER LANGHORNE *from* L. C., *crossing to up* R. D.

ALF.   Ah, Mr. Langhorne, going out for a stroll?

LANG.   Yah — yah, my deah boy. (*EXIT* R. U. E.)

> [ALFRED *quickly tries keys to door* R. 3, *and soon
> opens the door.   Careful to leave one key from bunch
> in the lock.   ENTER* EVANGELINE R. 3, *demurely.*

EVAN. (R. C.).   Wasn't it dreadful of mamma to lock
me in?

ALF. (L. C.).   Simply diabolical.   But do you happen to
remember, little dear, what it is that laughs at locks?
(*Takes* EVANGELINE'S *hand in his.*)

EVAN.   That laughs at locks?

ALF.   Yes.

EVAN. (*looking down; shakes head*).   No — I — I haven't
any idea.

ALF. Shall I tell you?

EVAN. (*looks at him*).   Perhaps you'd better not.

ALF.   Yes — but perhaps I'd better.   [*She looks up.*
It is love.

EVAN. (*looks on ground*).   Oh — (*looks at him*) I thought
love laughed at locksmiths, Mr. Hastings.

ALF. (*laughs*).   It laughs at anything, Evangeline, that
tries to keep us apart.

> [*Pause.* EVANGELINE *gets away and goes* R., *slightly
> embarrassed.   She turns suddenly and goes to*
> ALFRED.

EVAN.   Alfred — oh ! (*Covers mouth with hand. Bus.
of pretty embarrassment.*)

ALF. (*quickly*).   That's right — that's right ! (*Bus.*)

EVAN.   Listen.   Mamma locked me in.   It shows that
she's suspicious, and will come back any moment to look
after me.

ALF.   How very unfeeling on her part !

EVAN.   Oh, but that's the way mothers are, you know ;
so very suspicious and watchful.

ALF.   So it is — and I can't say I blame them very much

for it either; that is, I don't blame your mother. Why, if you belonged to me — (*pauses, looking into her eyes*).

EVAN. (*timidly*). If — if — I belonged to you?

ALF. (*with feeling*). If you were mine, little dear, my own, you know, and nobody's else, I'd be watchful too. Why, I'd be simply wretched every moment you were out of my sight.

EVAN. Would you?

ALF. Indeed, I would!

EVAN. How do you know?

ALF. (*low and earnest voice*). Because — because I am now (*slight pause*). So you see, it wouldn't be right for me to find fault with your mother for being watchful, would it?

EVANG. (*suddenly starting away*). No — and she is — dreadfully (*looks about anxiously*) — and we must be very careful. You stand there in that door (*pointing up* R., *going herself up to door* R. 3 E., *and* ALFRED *to up* R. D.), and I will stay close by this door. Then we can talk; and when you hear any one coming, I can run in, and you must be sure to lock the door just the way it was.

ALF. (*at door up* R.). Ah — but —

EVAN. (*at door,* R. 3 E.). Please! please! please! Any one coming?

　　　[*They take positions as* EVANGELINE *suggested.*
　　　READY bell L., *and voice up* R.

ALF. But, Evangeline — can't I come a little nearer?

EVAN. Oh, this is quite near! See (*reaches out hand*), you can reach my hand from there.

ALF. (*quickly catching her hand, and holding it*). So I can!

EVAN. Oh — I didn't mean for you to do it!

ALF. (*nearer to her*). My little darling! Have you thought of me once — since yesterday?

EVAN. (*after pause*). Hundreds and hundreds of times.

ALF. You have! (*Bus.; holds her in his arms.*)

EVAN. (*with some embarrassment*). Yes. Have you — thought of — of me any?

ALF. Thought of you! Will you believe me if I tell you how much?

EVAN. Oh, yes! I could never doubt your word — that is, if it is not too much, you know.

ALF. I'm afraid it is — if I should really tell you how much I've thought of you.

EVAN. Then perhaps you'd better not. But you might just tell me how many times; perhaps I would believe that.

ALF. How many times? [EVANGELINE *nods demurely*. How many times I've thought of you?

[EVANGELINE *same business*.

Only once.

EVAN. Once! (ALFRED *nods*.) Since yesterday!

ALF. Only once — since yesterday; for I've thought of nothing else, my little darling — and no one else — and so that one thought has lasted me the whole time.

[EVANGELINE, *reconciled, allows him to draw her close again*.

EVAN. O Alfred! I cannot bear to think we are to leave London in only a few weeks.

ALF. What matter, my little love — I shall follow you, wherever you go. [*READY* TOM *to enter* R. U. D.

EVAN. Will you? I — I don't know how it is, but even on the second day we came here, it seemed as if we had known each other for hundreds and hundreds of years. You were so good — so kind — and so, of course — I liked you very much — you see.

[*READY* BENDER *to enter up* R.

ALF. Liked me? Ah — but don't you — just a little more than like — just a little? [*Bus.* EVANGELINE *embarrassed*.

EVAN. (*low voice*). I like you — very much — of course —

ALF. How much? Enough to make it love — just a little love?

EVAN. (*pause: bus.*).   I'm afraid so.

ALF. (*holding her*).   You dear!   (*Holding* EVANGELINE'S *hand.*)   [EVANGELINE *suddenly, on reflecting what she has said, buries her face on* ALFRED'S *bosom, in confusion.*

(*Aside.*) Merciful heavens! What have I been saying?

ENTER TOM, R. U. D.

TOM.   All the Comforts of Home! (*Perceives them.*) Beg parding!

EXIT, R. U. D. ALFRED *and* EVANGELINE *start away from each other quickly.*

EVAN.   Did he see that I — that you — that we —?

ALF.   No — I don't think he saw it.   But I have a better idea than the one you had a while ago.   There's Langhorne's room — no one in it.   Window commands view of street — we can chat there, and see the moment any one comes near the house.   (*He holds out his hand.*)

EVAN.   That is a good place.   (*Takes his hand, and they both skip quickly into room up* L., *and stand or sit near the window, so that they are in sight of the audience.   They converse.*)   *ENTER* BENDER *suddenly, door up* R., *breathing as if he had come in a violent hurry.*

BEND. (C.).   I've escaped!   That is to say, by some unfortunate accident I lost my wife in the crowd.   (*Looks at* FIFI'S *door.*)   That money!   There's only one way — I must raise it on Josephine's diamonds.   She scarcely ever wears them — and I'll write Bleecker for the money, and get them out again before she notices it.   (*Goes down to door* R. 3.)   But the devil of it is, what Evangeline will say.   If I could only get her out of the room on some pretext or other!   (*Listens at door.*)   She seems to be asleep.   My soul — that would be fortunate!   (*He opens door very cautiously and looks in.*)   Why, she isn't there!   (*Looks about.*)   All the better — all the better!   (*EXIT into room* R. 3.)

[*Bell rings outside* L., *in* DABNEY'S *room.   Pause.*

Bell rings again in DABNEY'S *room. ENTER* BENDER R. 3, *with a jewel case which he tries to conceal under his coat.*

There, ha! ha! Burglarizing my own room! But where the deuce can Evangeline be? I'll lock the door — for I'll be back immediately. (*Locks door, taking key out.*) How careless, to leave the house open like this! Some one might have got in as easy as not, and stolen these diamonds, and then what in the devil's name would I have done? (*He goes up* R., *putting key in his pocket.*)

VOICE (*up-stairs, up* R.) Is anybody there?

BEND. (*starting, frightened*). Ough! Oh, Lord! (*Bus. of recovering. Speaks up-stairs.*) Yes; what do you want?

VOICE (*up-stairs, up* R.). I want to know what time it is?

BEND. The devil take him!

VOICE (*up-stairs, up* R.). I want to set my watch.

[*READY* THOMPSON *and* BAILIFF *to enter up* R.

BEND. (*calling up-stairs*). Well, set it back three-quarters of an hour. (*EXIT* BENDER, *up* R.)

[*Bell rings long and continuously in* DABNEY'S *room, outside* L. 2. *READY* TOM *to enter up* R.

ALF. (L. C.; *coming down into room, followed by* EVANGELINE). Good heavens! What a fiendish disturbance that fellow in there makes!

EVAN. (R. C.). What did you give him such an unearthly bell for?

ALF. The only one I could find. By Jove — a good idea! Do you know how they go to work to muffle a bell?

EVAN. Why, yes; just tie a piece of flannel around the tongue.

ALF. I will proceed to muffle Dabney's bell. (*Squeezes* EVANGELINE'S *hand.*) Be back in a minute, darling. (*EXIT* L. 2.) [*MUSIC. Ag. pp., louder, for bus., door locked. Play until stop cue.*

Evan. (C.; *going* R., *and stopping near door* R. 3). He loves me! He loves me! And I — I love him too! Yet there is something he is keeping from me — I can see that! Oh, I would be very happy — if I were sure — (*meditates sadly; suddenly happy again. Going to door* R. 3). But if he loves me — what else could I want? (*She tries to open door. Startled at finding it fastened.*) Locked! (*Tries again.*) Locked; and the key gone! Oh, dear! (*Frightened; she looks about.*) If mamma should come! Alfred — Mr. Hastings, I mean! (*Starts — listening.*) Oh, I hear some one coming! What shall I do? (*She darts to* L. C., *and suddenly turns into* LANGHORNE'S *room up* L. C., *and shuts door.*)

ENTER THOMPSON *up* R., *with* BAILIFF.
[*Stop music.*

THOMPSON (C.; *coming into room followed by* BAILIFF). This is where 'e lives, sir, and there's 'is room. I was in ere this morning, and found hout.

[*READY* ALFRED, *to enter* L. 2 E.

BAILIFF (R. C.; *crosses to* C.). Very well, where's my warrants? (BAILIFF *business a moment, getting out papers.*)

ENTER TOM *up* R., *crossing behind them, and down to* L. C. *hastily, with mustard plaster and pail of steaming hot water.* BAILIFF *and* THOMPSON *start toward* LANGHORNE'S *door.* TOM *runs quickly against them with pail of hot water, spilling some water.*

BAILIFF.
THOMPSON.   TOM.

TOM (L. C.). I begs your pardon, gents; but what's wantin'?

THOMP. (R. C.). We've come 'ere to attach Mr. Langhorne's things.

TOM. Ge-Whiffles! Well, I likes that!

BAIL. (C.). We're werry glad as you likes it, young man. So if you please, stand out o' the way.

[*READY* JOSEPHINE, *to enter up* R.

Tom. (*Bus. Slight threatening motion with pail of hot water; may simply set it in front of him*). Oh, it's that, is it? But supposin' I don't please?

Bail. (*loud voice*). You'd interfere with the law, would ye?

Tom. Oh, no! But afore you gits away with everything, I'd just make certain as we had enough o' Langhorne's luggage to settle up our little rent.

Bail. (*loud voice*). Look 'ere. I don't know nothink about your little rent, nor do I care.

> [Bailiff *and* Thompson *drop down* R. *in front of table.*

Tom (*loud*). I see you don't; an' it makes me have to do all the carin' myself — so — *ENTER* Alfred L. 2.

Tom.

Bailiff.   Alfred.

Thompson.

Alf. What's all this row about?

Bail. I've a warrant 'ere to attach the property of one Langhorne.

Tom. One Langhorne? That's all there is — ef ye was leavin' us another, I wouldn't care.

Alf. (*goes up toward* Tom). No use, Tom — we've got to submit.

Tom. An' let 'em take everything, sir?

Alf. No other way, my boy. (*Trying to persuade* Tom *to move away from door. They remonstrate with each other. Pantomine bus.*

> *ENTER* Josephine *up* R., *excited and breathless.*

Josephine (*bustling into room, down* C.). Where is my husband? Have you seen my husband, I say?

Thomp. (*to whom the remark seemed to be addressed*). No; an' I don't want to see 'im, neither.

> [Bailiff *and* Thompson *up* R. *of table, and over to* Tom, L.

Jos. (*going excitedly about*, R.).   To leave me in that way
— in the middle of a crowded street — with teams and om-
nibuses — and — and — oh !   (*Angry exclamation.   Stamps
foot.*)

BAILIFF.   TOM.

JOSEPHINE.

THOMPSON.

ALFRED.

BAIL.   Come — I can't wait here !

TOM (*at* D. L. C., *over* ALFRED'S *shoulder*).   There ain't
no one asked ye to.

ALF. (L. *of* TOM).   See here, Tom —

TOM.   Just let me drop this 'ere hot water down the back
of his neck, and decorate his cheek with a mustard plaster.

ALF. (*pulling* TOM *out of the way, and putting him over to
his* L.).   It's no use, I tell you — they can lock us up if we
interfere.

TOM (*discouraged; going one side*).   An' I gits 'alf !

ALF.   There, gentlemen.   (*He opens door of* LANGHORNE'S
room, L. C.)   You can go on with your — (*Sudden start.
Shuts door with slam, and stands before it.*)   Death and
Destruction !   Evangeline !

[JOSEPHINE *turns at bus., and looks.   Tableau.*

DOOR.

ALFRED.

BAILIFF.   TOM.

THOMPSON.

JOSEPHINE.

TOM (*down* L. ; *aside*).   Ge-Whiffles !   Wonder what struck
'im then ?

BAIL. (*up* C.).   Say, are we goin' hin, or not?

ALF. (*up* L. C.).   Not just now.   (*Glances at* JOSEPHINE.)

THOMP. (R. *of* BAILIFF).   What's the reason we can't ?

ALF.   The — the room isn't in order yet.

Jos. (*aside*). Oh, what delicacy!

Bail. Well, we'll put it in order mighty quick. (*Advances a step.*)

Alf. (*motions him back*). Stop! Wait!

[*READY muffled bell, L.*
(Alfred *comes forward a little.*) What's the amount of your claim?

Thomp. (R. *of* Alfred). Eight pound twelve and six-pence. (*Produces bill.*)

Alf. (*pulling money from pockets*). I'll settle the thing. It cleans me out, but I'll settle it.

Tom (*down* L., *putting pail of water on desk,* L.; *aghast; aside*). Oh, he's gone way off his head!

Thomp. Very well, sir. (*Takes money.*) Am much obliged — the receipt, sir. (*Going up* R.)

[*Bus. of* Tom *with plaster sticking to his hand.*

Alf. (L. C.). Now, kindly — (*indicating door*).

Bail. (C. *to* Alfred). But you've forgotten one little matter, my friend. There's costs to be settled afore I goes. One pound ten and six, sir, if you please.

Alf. Oh, the deuce! See here, my man, I haven't got it. Can't you —

Bail. No, I can't. So just stand aside now.

[Bailiff *advances toward door up* L. C., *and is stopped by* Alfred, *who stands before it.*

Jos. Stop! (*She goes to* Bailiff, *feeling in her pockets. Bus. of paying* Bailiff.) I will not see such delicacy of sentiment trodden under foot. Here! Take your miserable costs!

Alf. But, my dear Mrs. Bender —

Jos. Not a word! I prefer to do it.

Alf. (*aside*). By Jove, if the old girl knew what she was paying for!

Bail. (*having counted money, etc.*). Now we're all right, I believe. (*Starts* R. *with* Thompson.)

Tom. Oh, yes, you're all right! (*Follows them*, R.)   But
where do we come in?

> [*EXEUNT* BAILIFF *and* THOMPSON *up* R.   *Pause.*
> *A peculiar and unearthly sound of muffled bell comes*
> *from* DABNEY'S *room*, L. 2. (NOTE. *Experiment*
> *to get an effective and laughable sound for this.*)
> TOM, *who is up* R., *turns in surprise*. ALFRED
> *and* JOSEPHINE *also listen.*

(*Starting toward* DABNEY'S *room*, L. 2.)   Well, ef his bell
ain't done an' took a spasm now! (TOM *seizes water-pail*
and plaster, and rushes off L. 2. *As he goes.*)   Comin' sir —
comin'! Comin'! (*EXIT*, L. 2.)

Jos. (R. C. *to* ALFRED).   I admire your delicacy so much,
Mr. Hastings.   [*READY knock*, L. C.

ALF. (L. C.).   Thanks! Thanks! But I — I really can't
help it; it is an inborn instinct with me, madam. (*Trying*
to keep her away from door up L. C.)

Jos. (R. C.).   Yes; but I don't know many people who
would be willing to pay so much for a mere sentiment.   Is
the gentleman's apartment really in such disorder?   Let me
just peep in. (*Turns as if to go to the door up* L. C.)

ALF. (*with a start*).   No! (*Stands between her and the*
door L. C.)   Ah — that is — really, Mrs. Bender — consider
my feelings!   [JOSEPHINE *looks at* ALFRED *an instant.*

Jos. (*aside*).   How he started!   It can't be possible there's
any — I really begin to suspect that, after all — (*A frown*
appears upon her face slowly.   Turns to ALFRED.   *Voice*
changed to harder tone.)   Mr. Hastings, I shall have to insist upon looking into that room.

ALF.   Insist?   Come now — that's hardly the thing, is it,
for one who appreciates my delicacy of sentiment?

                         [*READY* LANGHORNE, *to enter up* R.

Jos.   Delicacy, sir, has nothing to do with it now.   I
am living beneath your roof with my family — my husband
— and my daughter — (*on "daughter," points to room* R. 3.)

[ALFRED *gives a slight start.*

If I became convince'd that everything was not as it should be, I would instantly quit the house.

ALF.   Surely, you do not suspect —

JOS.   From your actions, Mr. Hastings, I know that there is some one in that room you wish to conceal.   As you do not choose to relieve my mind at once by opening the door, it more than confirms my suspicions.   I shall therefore wait here until the person — whoever it is — comes out.   (*Seats herself in a chair, back to audience,* L. *of* R. *table.*)   It is a duty I owe my family.

> [ALFRED *simply stares blankly at* JOSEPHINE.   *After watching* JOSEPHINE *seat herself, he pulls newspaper from pocket.   Draws chair before door up* L. C., *and reads.*

(*Aside.*)   If he thinks that affects my mind, he is the most mistaken individual on this quarter of the globe.

> [JOSEPHINE *begins to hum a song, her indignation showing in it.*   ALFRED *takes it up, whistling softly.*   JOSEPHINE *stops angrily, and looks daggers.   A soft knock on door up* L. C., *from within.*
> *READY* BENDER, *to enter up* R.

ALF. (*aside*).   The devil!   Now Evangeline wants to get out.   (*Coughs, and hitches around in his chair as if to cover up the sound made by* EVANGELINE.)

> *ENTER* LANGHORNE *up* R., *running in hastily, as if pursued.*

LANG. (*coming in*).   If that woman saw me. I am lost! (*Going to* ALFRED.   *Stops, seeing situation.*)

> [*READY* EVANGELINE *to enter up* L.

ALF. (*at door* L. C.; *aside*).   Merciful Powers!   Now he'll want to get in.   [JOSEPHINE *starts, and watches eagerly.*

LANG. (*on* ALFRED'S R., *going quickly to door*).   You will permit me?

ALF. (*quickly, in an undertone to* LANGHORNE).   For

Heaven's sake, don't! There's a woman in there who must not be seen.

LANG. (*to* ALFRED). But see heah, deah boy—there's a woman after me, and I mustn't be seen.

ALF. (*to* LANGHORNE). Go into my room.

LANG. Your—oh—certainly! (*Starts down* R.) I don't care where I go, ye know, as long as I go somewhere. (*Dodges around* JOSEPHINE'S *chair*). Aw—chawming day! (*EXIT* R. 2.)

JOS. (*aside*). It's a conspiracy!

                    ENTER BENDER *up* R., *rushing in.*

BEND. Ha, ha! Thank Heaven, I've fixed that! (*Sees* JOSEPHINE. *Instantly turns square about, and starts toward door up* R. *again, and EXIT door up* R.)

JOS. (*rising quickly*). Theodore! Theodore! Stop, I say! (*She follows* BENDER.) Stop! I wish to speak with you. Theodore! (*EXIT, door up* R.)

ALF. (*aside*). Thank Heaven for that! (*Opens door up* L.) Evangeline, quick!   *ENTER* EVANGELINE, *up* L. Quick, quick! To your room! (*Passing her across to* R.)

        [EVANGELINE *starts toward* R. 3. *ENTER* JOSE-
        PHINE *and* BENDER, *up* R. JOSEPHINE *sees* EVAN-
        GELINE, *and stands in horror for an instant.*

JOS. (*up* R. C.; *on seeing* EVANGELINE). What! (*Almost a scream.*)   [*All stand on tableau.*

ALF. (L., *having fallen on ottoman; aside*). Lost!

BEND. (*up* R.; *aside*). Hullo! (*Looks about to see what it is.*)

                BENDER.   JOSEPHINE.
                    EVANGELINE.
                            ALFRED.

JOS. (R. C.). Then you were there?

EVAN. (L. C.). Yes, mamma.

        [ALFRED *starts as if to speak.* EVANGELINE *motions*
        him not to.

No, Alfred, I will tell them.

BEND. "Alfred!" (*Coming down* R.)

JOS. (*up* R. C.). "Alfred!"

EVAN. (C.). I had been chatting with Alfred, and I hid in that room when I heard you coming. I will not and cannot deny it.

BEND. (R.; *aside, admiringly*). What courage the girl has!

JOS. (*up* R. C.). And you have the hardihood to speak of this so calmly! What — what does it mean?

EVAN. (*up* L. C.). It means, mamma, that Alfred and I love each other. He has told me so, and I have told him so — and that's all there is about it.

> [*READY* FIFI, *to enter* L. 3 E.

BEND. (*down* R.; *aside*). Magnificent! Such coolness! (*Speaks aloud without thinking, clapping hands together.*) Bravo!

JOS. (*turning upon him*). Theodore! (JOSEPHINE *unlocks door* R. 3 E.)

> [BENDER *collapses, but recovers, and claps hands together behind his back, where* JOSEPHINE *cannot see him.*

(*To* EVANGELINE.) Go to your room at once! What course I shall take with you, I do not yet know.

. EVAN. (*giving* ALFRED *her hand*). Until we meet again, Alfred dear!

> [JOSEPHINE *opens door* R. 3, *and stands.* EXIT EVANGELINE *calmly* R. 3, *turning at door, and throwing a kiss seriously and tenderly to* ALFRED.

BEND. Ha, ha! (*Chuckles — not a laugh. Crosses up to* ALFRED, L. C.)

JOS. (*at door*, R. 3 E.). Theodore!

> [BENDER *becomes serious at once.*

I have a few words to say to you soon. (*EXIT* R. 3, *after giving* BENDER *a look of great significance.*)

> [*READY* DABNEY *and* TOM, *to enter* L. 2 E.

BEND. (R. C., *to* ALFRED L. C., *slapping him on the shoulder*).

That's a woman — eh? Now — now you can have some idea of how I feel — ha, ha, ha!

> *MUSIC. Lively music, with comedy element very predominant. Play pp. during dialogue, increasing to a little louder near end of act, and forte for curtain.* FIFI *opens door* L. 3.

FIFI. Mr. Bender!

BEND. Eh?

FIFI. The costume has come. Do you want to see me as Prince Vladimir?

BEND. The costume? (*Giving a glance towards door* R. 3.) Perfectly delighted, my dear! (BENDER *hastens toward* FIFI.) *ENTER* FIFI, L. 3, *in costume of Prince Vladimir.* Ha, ha, ha! Charming! charming!

FIFI. How do you like it, Mr. Bender?

> [*Just as* BENDER *reaches the table near* R. C., JOSE- PHINE *ENTERS* R. 3.

JOS. (*up* R., *above the table*). Now, Theodore, I would like to know —

> [ALFRED, *up* C., *gives quick exclamation of alarm.*

BEND. (C.; *just above the* L. *of table ; terrified*). Ah! (*He quickly snatches table-cover from table near* C., *and raises it high in the air, so that* FIFI *is hidden from view.*) My dear have you noticed the beautiful pattern on this table-cover? Simply divine! Exquisite! Adorable!

> [ALFRED, *up* C., *seizes* FIFI *on table-cover bus., and hurries her off at* L. 3 *an instant later. ENTER* EVANGELINE, *door* R. 3. *She stands at the door, trying to see what causes the excitement.* JOSE- PHINE, *on table-cover bus., stands astonished. At table-cover bus. and exclamations, etc., enter* DAB- NEY L. 2 E. DABNEY *is swaddled up with flan- nels, etc., as if for illness. Mustard-plaster on chest, old dressing-gown, stocking-feet, etc.*
>
> *MUSIC. A little louder, but still well down.*

DAB. (L. C.; *seeing* FIFI *as* ALFRED *hurries her off*). Ah! (*Half shriek.*) That creature sang in my opera, and she —

ALF. (*up* C.; *quick shout to* TOM). Stop him!

    (*ENTER* TOM L. 2 E. *He carries plaster, bandages, etc.*)

TOM. (L.; *jumping on* DABNEY). Quite right, sir.

                    [*READY curtain.*

    MUSIC. Forte for curtain. TOM *throws arms around* DABNEY'S *neck, head, etc., so that he is effectively silenced, and they fall upon the ottoman together,* DABNEY *uttering muffled yells and shrieks,* TOM *putting plaster over his mouth.* ALFRED *snatches up newspaper, and stands reading nonchalantly before door* L. 3. BENDER *drops, overcome, into chair up* C., *the table-cover falling over him.* JOSEPHINE, R., *or* R. C., *transfixed with astonishment at the behavior of the gentlemen.* (NOTE. *All this business at climax to occupy only an instant.*)

                    [*RING curtain.*

CURTAIN.

ACT III.

SCENE. — Same as in Act I. Some trifling changes in furniture can be made to advantage. Anything that will tend to make a little change will perhaps relieve the monotony.

> *MUSIC. — Comedy bit for rise of curtain. Lively, and somewhat adapted to* TOM'S *business. Come to pp. when curtain is up. Stop on beginning of* TOM'S *speech.*

> TOM *discovered working down near* C., *at a large shallow pasteboard box, the empty interior of which is exposed to view of audience. He appears to have been glueing something on bottom, which is turned up stage. READY* BENDER, *to enter* R. 3 E. *READY bell, off* L. 2 E.

TOM (*seated* L. *of* R. *table*).   I've had enough o' that there cove as yells down them stairs ev'ry other minit, a-wanting ter know what time it is, an' I'm a-goin' ter fix him so's he won't give us no more trouble.   Ef he goes on with it, the nervous galoot in there's a-goin' ter leave, an' he'll burst up the whole business afore we know it — an' I ain't goin' ter have the business bursted now (*bus. working*) — while I gits half.   (*Bus. with box.   He picks up box, rushes up* R., *then, suddenly turning box so that bottom is to front, he quickly hangs it to a hook on wall near foot of stairs, and immediately rushes down and to table* C., *where he gets a pot of black paint and brushes, waiting for laugh, if any, on audience seeing back of box.   On back of box is painted or pasted a white paper or cardboard, with an enormous clock face painted upon it, without any hands.* TOM *dashes up with the paint, and quickly paints from six to ten hands on the clock, these hands pointing in every direc-*

tion. He names the time of each as he puts it in. Bus.) Quarter-past eleving. (*Bus.*) Two minutes afore three. (*Bus.*)
Seving o'clock. (*Etc.*) There! now he can take his choice
— an' no noise about it. (*Stands up* R., *viewing his work.*)
That there ain't so bad, now. When I gits through with this
here job, I kin go into the clock business.

> [*READY bell and noise above, up* R.
> *ENTER* BENDER, R. 3. *He is in good spirits, and
> comes on whistling. Stops and looks at the clock
> face and at* TOM.

What do you think of it, sir?

BEND. (R.). Is that style of timepiece your own invention?   [*READY* ALFRED, *to enter* R. 2 E.

TOM (L.). It's fur the feller up-stairs, sir; him as makes
such a contineral hollerin' fur the time. He'd orter be out
now in a minit or two—it's more'n half an hour now sence
the last time.

BEND. Well, all I can say is—

> [*Bell rings in* DABNEY'S *room* L. 2. TOM *starts up
> R., but stops.*

TOM. Ge-Whiffles! I thought it was 'im. It was the
other one. (*Goes toward* L. 2.)   [*Bell rings above, up* R.

TOM *and* BEND. There! (TOM *and* BENDER *bus. of quick
start and look.*)

VOICE (*above; up* R.). Look here! Can't somebody down
there tell me what—

> [*Sudden jangle of bell, which comes banging and rat-
> tling down the stairs from above, followed by pipe,
> novel, and a beer mug; noise of furniture. TOM
> and BENDER bus. of holding in suppressed laughter.
> Finally burst out. If audience take it, keep up by
> BENDER falling into a chair, and TOM rolling on
> the floor.*

TOM (*on bus.*). That there settled 'im, sir.

BEND. That clock would settle anything. Ha, ha!

ENTER ALFRED *door* R. 2. *Hat, etc., as if from street.*

ALF. (R.; *after looking at bus.*). From appearances, one would suppose you were having quite a humorous time.

BEND. (C.). Ah, ha, ha, ha! (*Points to clock up* R.) For the benefit of the second floor!

ALF. (*crosses to* C.; *seeing clock*). Has the second floor seen it?

TOM. Yes, sir; he's just took an observation.
          [*Bell rings in* DABNEY'S *room outside* L. 2.
Ge-Whiffles! I forgot all about that nervous galoot. (*EXIT* L. 2.)

DAB. (*in room* L. 2 E.) Don't! don't!
          [BENDER *goes walking about room, smiling, and*
          whistling snatches of things out of tune, hands be-
          hind him, etc. Half smiling now and then, as if
          thinking of something very pleasant. ALFRED
          watches him a while.

ALF. (*to* L.; *aside*). The old boy is in great spirits to-day. Wonder what's going on. As he is to be my father-in-law, I'll have to look out for him a little. (*Looks at* BENDER.)
          [BENDER *goes up* R., *and looks off at door* R. 3 E.
Think of it! Engaged to that little dear — yes, and as good as engaged to my cousin Emily at the same time! A pretty position to be in! But I'm in it, and the only way is to tell Uncle Egbert the whole thing when he comes home; for I couldn't give up Evangeline. Oh, no! Anything but that!   [BENDER *comes down* C.
Anything but that!

BEND. (C.). Alfred, my boy, has the post come in this morning?

ALF. (L.). No, not yet.
          [BENDER *walks about up and down* R. ALFRED
          sticks his hands in his pockets and looks at him.
I say, you must be expecting something very nice.

BEND. (R. C.; *stops and looks at* ALFRED). I am. (*Goes near* ALFRED. *Speaks confidentially.*) Ha, ha! (*Chuckles.*) It's too good to keep.

ALF. Don't keep it, then.

BEND. The fact is (*glances around to see that no one overhears*), I'm expecting a letter — for my wife.

ALF. That is, she's expecting it?

BEND. No, no! Not by a — 'hem! (*Bus. Glance.*) She doesn't know anything about it.

ALF. Ah!

BEND. I — (*impressively, in* ALFRED'S *ear*). I wrote it myself; disguised hand, of course. Oh, she'll never know it's from me!

ALF. In that case, I've no doubt she'll be delighted to get it.

BEND. No, I hardly think so, as it informs her that I have an appointment to-day, at the park, near the marble arch.

ALF. It does! You mean —a lady?

[BENDER *nods emphatically, looking very jovial and pleased, and walks around a little, whistling.*

But, my dear Mr. Bender —

BEND. (R. C.). Perfectly true. (*Nods significantly.*) I have an appointment — but not at the park.

ALF. (L. C.). Where?

[*READY* JOSEPHINE, *to enter* R. 3 E.

BEND. (*confidentially*). Here.

ALF. By Jove! [BENDER *nods, and walks as before.* Who is the — the other party, if I may ask?

[BENDER *stops, turns to* ALFRED. *Motions significantly toward* FIFI'S *door,* L. 3.

Not — not the opera singer!

BEND. (*finger to lips*). Sh! Yes.

ALF. (*after regarding* BENDER *an instant*). How very rapid you are for an elderly man.

BEND. (R.; *pleased*). I — I did Miss Fifi a little favor, you know; and out of gratitude she has invited me to a — ahem — a champagne breakfast. That is, she furnishes the invitation, and I — furnish the breakfast.

ALF. And in the meantime, Mrs. Bender goes to waylay you?

BEND. (*taking* R.). At the marble arch.

> [ALFRED *stares in astonishment.* BENDER *pauses an instant, then paces restlessly up to* C. ALFRED *crosses to* R.

Now, what the deuce delays that mail?

> [*Door of room* R. 3 *opens.*

Careful, now!

> [BENDER *down, meeting* JOSEPHINE. *ENTER* JOSE-PHINE, *dressed for calling. Crosses down* L.

Why, Josephine, love, are you going — anywhere in particular?   [*READY* TOM, *to enter* L. 2 E.

JOS. (L.). Do you forget that we were to make several calls to-day with our dear Alfred and Evangeline?

ALF. (R.). Oh, Heavens!

> [*READY double knock, up* R. *door.*

BENDER.

ALFRED.

JOSEPHINE.

JOS. (L.). Alfred, dear, not dressed yet?

ALF. (R.). Well, it seemed to me — that — er — the weather —

JOS. Why, the weather is perfect.

ALF. Yes; but the — the reports say there's another blizzard on the way from America. (*Holding up a newspaper.*) Do you know what a frightful thing a blizzard from America is?

JOS. No; and I don't care. (*Severely.*) We are to make these calls.

[ALFRED *stands an instant looking at her.* BENDER
*smothers a laugh, but quickly catches himself, and
looks solemn.* ALFRED *turns and goes to door* R. 2.

ALF. (*at door* R. 2; *aside*). Anything but calling on her
relatives! (*Turns and looks at* JOSEPHINE. *She is still looking at him. He at once exits into his room* R. 2.)

JOS. (L.; *looks severely at* BENDER). Theodore, you are
to come with us.

BEND. (R.). I? Oh, of course — of course. (*Aside.*)
Now what is the matter with that d——d postman!

[*ENTER* TOM L. 2, *with a demijohn and several
bottles. He goes rapidly across, up* R.

JOS. Thomas! Thomas!

TOM (*up* R.). Yes'm — one minute, mum. (*Up* R., *and
puts things down. Turns to* JOSEPHINE.)

JOS. Come here.

TOM. I am here, mum.

[*Double knock of Postman, door up* R.

BEND. (*start of relief*). Tom — letters.

TOM (*going to door up* R.). Quite right, sir. (TOM *disap-
pears an instant. Returns at once.*)

[BENDER *fills time with a pleased smile and glance
at* JOSEPHINE.

(*Goes quickly to* BENDER.) Paper for you, sir. (*Down* C.)

BEND. (*alarmed*). Is that — all?

TOM (*goes to* JOSEPHINE). Letter fur you, mum. (*Goes
up* R. *and stands a moment.*)

[JOSEPHINE *takes it, and bus. of opening.*

BEND. (*sits* L. *of* R. *table, opening the paper, and looking
over the top at* JOSEPHINE; *aside, chuckling*). That's the one.

[JOSEPHINE *looks up.* BENDER *bus. of instantly opening and plunging into his paper.*

TOM (C.; *aside*). Ge-Whiffles! The old duck's got
somethin' on hand again; I kin tell it every time. (*EXIT
up* R. *to* L.)

Jos. (L.). What wretched writing! (*Reads.*)

Bend. (R. ; *aside*). Sorry she doesn't like it.

                [*READY* Alfred, *to enter* R. 2 E.

Jos. (*reads*). " Respected Madam. Pray do not consider me too presuming, but I think it my duty to — warn you." (*She looks closer, interested.*) What's this! (*Reads more excitedly, repeating aloud only the important parts.*) " At Hyde Park, Marble Arch, between ten and eleven o'clock — A well-meaning Friend." Ah ! (*Subdued gasp, dropping the letter to the floor.*)

       [Bender *has had his eye on* Josephine *over or under his paper during above.*

Bend. (*rises to* Josephine, *laying aside paper*). Now, what they wanted to send me that for — er — Good Heavens, Josephine ! (*As if noticing her strained expression.*) No unpleasant news, I hope ?

Jos. (L. ; *starts. Assumes a smile which is rather ghastly*). Oh, no. Very pleasant — very — ha, ha ! Yes.

Bend. (R., *as if suspicious*). Um ! Looks like a man's handwriting.

Jos. (*assumed indifference*). Does it ? (*Smiles.*)

Bend. (*assuming some warmth*). I said it did.

Jos. Oh — really !

       [Bender *makes a motion as if to pick the letter up ;* Josephine, *with sudden exclamation of alarm, snatches it from floor. They stand looking at each other. Tableau for an instant.*

Bend. (R. C.). There's something in that letter.

Jos. (L. C.). That's quite possible, as you didn't write it.

Bend. Your actions are very suspicious, madam. (*Bus.*) I'd have you understand that, as your husband, I have a right —

       ENTER Alfred, R. 2, *dressed for calling. He stops on seeing situation.*

(*Aside. Turning away. Chuckles.*)

Jos. (*crosses to* Alfred, R. *To* Alfred, *very pleasantly, yet showing the bitter feeling beneath*). Oh, Alfred, I have changed my plans a little; I feel a headache coming on — and (*glances at* Bender) —

JOSEPHINE.

ALFRED.

BENDER.

and — I think I'd better lie down quietly for a little while.

[*READY* Evangeline, *to enter* R. 3 E.

BEND. (*approaching* Josephine; *speaks sympathetically*). Oh, my dear Josephine, I —

[Josephine *shoots a glance at* Bender *which stops him instantly.*

Jos. (C.; *to* Alfred). You and Evangeline are to go to the Dickermans' without me, and I will call there for you later.

BEND. (L.). Oh, so we aren't to go with them? In that case, my dear, I will take the opportunity to call on an old business friend of mine in Upton Street.

Jos. (*looking calmly and stonily at* Bender). You will call on an old business friend of yours in Upton Street?

BEND. Yes. You remember Barton Briggs? Dear old fellow! Shall I give him your regards?

Jos. Oh, do. By all means. (*Showing savageness in spite of herself.*) Give the dear old fellow my regards.

[*READY* Tom, *to enter up* R.

BEND. (*crosses up to* R. U. D. *Cheerfully*). Yes, my angel, I will. Good-bye for a little while. (*EXIT up* R., *whistling or humming ; can get hat and cane up* R. *if he cannot easily arrange to bring them on at entrance.*)

Jos. (*taking* L.; *looking after him. Aside*). Oh, the hypocrite! (*Going up* C.)

ENTER Evangeline, R. 3, *very tastefully dressed.*
Alfred *to* C. Evangeline *down on his* R.

ALF. (*going quickly to* EVANGELINE). My little darling, how enchanting you look!

EVAN. (R. C.; *looking up to him; pleased*). Do I? (*Bus. with gloves, etc.*) But you ought not to say so, you know.

ALF. (C.). Can't help it. (ALFRED *glances at* JOSEPHINE, *and seeing her turned away, steals a kiss from* EVANGELINE. *Bus.*)   [JOSEPHINE *turns quickly and comes down* L.

EVAN. (R. C.). Where is papa?

JOS. (L.; *significantly*). He has gone to call upon a dear old business friend.

EVAN. (R.). But I thought —

[*READY* BENDER, *to enter up* R.

JOS. No matter what you thought. Come — we will start. (*Goes up* R. *a little.*)

ALF. (C.). Start! Aren't you going to lie down after all?   [ALFRED *and* EVANGELINE *go up* R.

JOS. I have decided it would be better for me to take the air.

ALF. Oh!

[JOSEPHINE *suddenly turns, as if she had thought of something. Marches down to her door,* R. 3, *and reaching in, gets an umbrella. ENTER* TOM *up* R. *from* L. *He comes down a little* L., *looking at the party.* ALFRED *and* EVANGELINE *watch* JO-SEPHINE'S *movements.* JOSEPHINE *walks back up* R., *carrying umbrella with peculiar fierceness of manner.* TOM, *who was coming slowly down, slides back off to* L. C., *watching* JOSEPHINE *with evident concern.*

EVAN. (*surprised*). But, mamma, dear, you don't want an umbrella to-day!

TOM.

D. R. 3. E., JOSEPHINE.

EVANGELINE.   ALFRED.

Jos. (*turning at door up* R.)   Oh, I don't know about that. The report says there's a blizzard coming from America, and it's just as well to be prepared. (*Marches out up* R., *gripping the umbrella ferociously.*)

Evan. (*looking at* Alfred).   What does she mean, Alfred?

Alf.   She means business.

[*EXEUNT* Alfred *and* Evangeline, *up* R.

Tom (*gives a whistle indicative of "whew!"*).   Ge-Whiffles, but ef it's old Bender she's got in her mind, they'll have to bring 'im 'ome in baskets!   (*EXIT, up* R. *to* L.)

ENTER Bender, *door up* R.

Bend. (*coming* C.).   Everything is working like a charm! My wife safely down the street, and making a bee-line for Hyde Park.   I hope she'll enjoy the walk.   If she doesn't — 'hem — perhaps she'll enjoy the walk back. (*Chuckles.*)

ENTER Tom *up* R., *from* L., *with two bottles of champagne.   Crossing to door* L. 2 E.

Ah, Tom!   (*Meeting* Tom *up* L. C.)

Tom (L. C.).   Yes, sir!

Bend. (R. C.).   They are to send in a little breakfast from Torino's.   When it comes, take care of it.

[*READY knock and* Voice *up* R. D.

Tom (L. C.).   I've had breakfast, sir.

Bend. (R. C.).   No, no!   It's for Miss Oritanski.   Ha, ha! (*Chuckles.*)   I am invited to join her.   I say — I suppose there's no objection — to — 'hem — a — quiet little breakfast here?

Tom.   None whatsomever, sir.   We aims to give our lodgers "all the comforts of home."

Bend.   Good!   When it comes, just take it to her room.

Tom.   She locked it up, sir, when she went out.

Bend. (*thunderstruck*).   Went — went out!

Tom.   Yes, sir.

Bend.   Where?

Tom.   To the theatre, sir.   She had a sudden call for re-

hearsal — somebody sick. She told me to tell you as she
was werry sorry indeed — werry sorry.

BEND. Why — confound it — I was to breakfast with her!
Why — (*is speechless with vexation*).

[*Knock outside, up* R. TOM *rushes up* R., *and EXIT* R.
That's probably the breakfast. What infernal, confounded,
outrageous luck!

> [*READY* ALFRED *to enter up* R. C. *ENTER* TOM
> *with breakfast hamper, which he sets near* FIFI's
> *door,* L. 3, *on a chair. This hamper should contain
> two bottles of champagne (one may be a dummy),
> some very fancily done up French chops, a salad
> dressed in the highest style of art, and other fancy
> dishes. Rolls, wine-glasses, knives, plates, nap-
> kins, etc., for two ; and two bunches of flowers for
> button-hole and corsage. The salads and fancy
> dishes may be dummies ; chops, rolls, champagne,
> and two or three small things should be practical
> for business.*

(*Looking dubiously at the breakfast.*) What the deuce can
I do?

TOM (*coming down* L.). Ef it wuz me, sir, I'd hop into a
cab an' drive to the theatre.

BEND. Good idea. (*Goes up* R.) I'll do it. (*EXIT
quickly up* R.)

TOM (L. C., *looking after* BENDER). Ef he'd a seen his
ole lady a-goin' out with that there umbrella o' hern, he'd
be takin' a cab for the railway station.

[*Knock up* R. D. TOM *goes up to* D. R. *and EXIT.*

VOICE (*outside*). Telegram, sir.

TOM (*outside*). Telegram?

VOICE (*outside*). Yes,. sir.

> *ENTER* TOM *with telegram, up* R.

TOM (*down* L. C., *reads address*). To Alfred Hastin's, Esq.
Ge-Whiffles! Ef people aint commencin' a-telegraphin' fur

rooms! This here house is gittin' pop'lar. (*Puts envelope in his pocket.*)   *ENTER* ALFRED *hastily, up* R.

ALF. (R. C.). See here, Tom! Miss Bender dropped her bracelet — she thinks it was in this room. Help me look, quick!

TOM (I. C.). Yes, sir.

> [ALFRED *and* TOM *look about on floor.*

ALF. (R., *seeing envelope sticking out of* TOM's *pocket*). What have you got there?

TOM (L., *quickly handing envelope — innocent and official manner, as if he had just arrived with it*). Telegram for you, sir.

ALF. (*snatching and opening it*). Good Heavens, why didn't you say so!

TOM. I did, sir. I just said so.

> [ALFRED *hastily opens, and reads telegram. READY bell*, L.

ALF. Good Heavens!

> [TOM *stares at* ALFRED *an instant.*

TOM (*without emotion*). Anybody dead, sir?

ALF. Yes — we're dead.

TOM. W'en is the funeral?

ALF. You'd better get ready for it now. My aunt is coming home. (*Reads dispatch.*) "Sent from Venice. Mr. Pettibone gone to Hamburg on business. Am coming home with Emily. Must see you. Very important matter. Rosabelle Pettibone." (*Sits down on chair* R., *overcome.*)

> [TOM *goes and sits on the ottoman*, I.

(ALFRED *suddenly jumps up.*) Here — get me some paper — quick now — no time to waste.

> (ALFRED *takes stylographic pen from his pocket.*)

TOM (*jumping up*). Yes, sir! (*Snatches paper, etc., from desk*, L. *Bus.*)   [*READY* FIFI, *to enter up* R.

ALF. (*seated* L. *of* R. *table*). I'll try to stop them. Not much chance, but I'll try. (*Writes quickly, reading aloud.*)

"Mrs. Egbert Pettibone, Venice. In mercy's sake, don't come. Impossible. Dangerous. House — _(Thinks.)_ What the devil can I say is the matter with the house?

Tom. Burnt down.

Alf. Hang it, they'd come all the sooner!

Tom. Blown up. _(Bell L. 2 E.)_ Oh, that nervous galoot has ordered more wine. _(Tom rushes off with the two bottles, L. 2 E.)_

Alf. Oh, no — no. Ah! _(Writes rapidly.)_ "House just painted. Painter's colic. Pipes burst. Influenza epidemic. Small-pox next door. Alfred." _(Bus.)_ Here, quick, Tom! _ENTER_ Tom L. 2 E. Telegraph office! _(Rising and hurrying Tom up toward door R.)._ Run all the way!

Tom _(starts up R.)._ Yes, sir. _(Stops C.)_ Pay it, sir?

Alf. No, hang it! Collect.

Tom. Correct! _(EXIT door up R.)_

Alf. They'll never get it. _(Looks at his telegram.)_ N — probably started already. Only one thing to do. Get our lodgers out — and Evangeline — and Emily — _(Crosses to L.)_ Oh, the deuce! _(Turns to C.)_ And how in Heaven's name I am to evict my parents-in-law, is more than I —

ENTER Fifi _door up R., coming down L. C., jauntily dressed. A little love of a bonnet, gloves, etc._

(Aside.) And here's another one. Oh, Lord, if my aunt should find her here! _(Crosses to R.)_ I must get her out first.

Fifi _(L. C., very bright and vivacious)._ Ah, Doctor, how charmed I am to meet you! _(Begins to take off gloves.)_

Alf. _(R. C.)._ Thanks, I'm sure.

Fifi. Dear me! _(Imitating his tone.)_ "Thanks, I'm sure." Something gone wrong with my fascinating landlord?

Alf. Your fascinating landlord has a confession to make.

Fifi _(in mock alarm, motioning him to stop with one hand,_

and going toward her door). Mercy, please don't, doctor! (*Takes key and unlocks door* L. 3.) At least not until I've had something to sustain me. This dreadful rehearsal made me miss a most delightful breakfast that — (*Sees hamper near her door. Goes to it.*) Ah! (*Delighted.*) Why, it's here! Poor Mr. Bender! (*Laughs merrily.*) He couldn't wait.

ALF. But, my dear Miss Oritanski —

FIFI (*almost screams with sudden idea*). Oh, stop! You shall breakfast with me.

ALF. But, my dear Miss Oritanski —

FIFI. There — there — that will do. That table (*pointing up* C.), bring it down here.

> [*Business.* FIFI *stamps foot.* ALFRED *does not notice what she says.*

FIFI. Bring that table here. [ALFRED *drags table down as if not knowing what he is doing, all the time trying to speak. Through the whole scene* ALFRED *acts as if unconscious of what he is about. No sign of the slightest enjoyment or spirit appears. Acts mechanically.*

> (FIFI *places hamper on ottoman, instantly going to work to get things out, throwing table-cloth to* ALFRED.)

Spread it out — spread it out!　　　　　 [ALFRED *does so.* And then you can confess all you like. An immense saving of time. Breakfast — confess — all in one.

ALF. (R. *of the table; going nearer*). But, my dear young lady — (*Back of the ottoman.*)

FIFI (*pushing something into his hand*). Just put that there. (*Flies about. Bus. quick. Vivacious.*)

ALF. (*puts article in wrong place on table, not knowing where*). You don't understand — what I was going to —

FIFI. No, no! not there. There! (*Changes it.*) Oh, dear! you're not much assistance, I must say! That goes there. (*Bus. of putting another article into his hand.*) That's it! You actually got that right!

ALF. (*bus.*). Now, Miss Oritanski, — listen. This is a matter of vital importance.

FIFI. If you want a matter of vital importance, open this (*tossing bottle of champagne to* ALFRED, *and corkscrew from hamper*).

ALF. (*catches bottle*). But look here, there's no time to lose.

FIFI. Well — I'm not losing any, am I ?

ALF. (*aside*). By Jove, I should say not ! (*Holds bottle mechanically, as he caught it.*)

FIFI. You're the one that's losing time. Why don't you open it ?

ALF. Open what ?   [FIFI *points to bottle.*
Oh, you want that opened ?

FIFI. Of course, Mr. Stupid.

ALF. But first —

FIFI. Nothing first. I won't hear a word, unless you do as I say.

ALF. Oh, Lord ! (*Opens bottle as if it were a nuisance.*)

FIFI (*gets chair from up* C. *and pushes* ALFRED *into it* R. *of table ; then kneels herself on back of the ottoman close to the* L. *of table*). That's it ! you're coming to your senses at last.

                    [*READY* EVANGELINE, *to enter up* R.

ALF. (*bus. with bottle*). On the contrary, I am losing them.

FIFI.

OTTOMAN.

ALFRED.   TABLE.

FIFI. There ! (*Finishes setting table.*)

ALF. But you said you'd listen if —

FIFI. There ! (*Bus. of delicately giving* ALFRED *a French chop with her fingers.*) Just try this. It's from Torino's. I know it by the style.

                    [ALFRED, *confused an instant, holds chop.*
Eat it. You don't know how nice it is.

[ALFRED *seated, confused, with the chop in one hand, and champagne bottle in the other.*

Pour the wine, why don't you ? [ALFRED *pours wine in glass.* Pour it ! Ah, isn't that lovely ! You'll feel better in a moment.

ALF. (*aside*). Good Heavens — I must stop this !

ENTER EVANGELINE *up* R. *Stops horrified, on seeing* ALFRED *and* FIFI.

MUSIC. — Pathetic ; sympathetic ; pp. again until stop cue.

FIFI (*holding up glass of champagne*). Happy days, doctor !

ALF. But first —

EVANGELINE.

FIFI.

ALFRED. TABLE. OTTOMAN.

FIFI. No, no ! Happy days first ! Happy days, doctor ! then, perhaps, I'll listen.

ALF. (*quickly, as if to get through with it*). Happy days, then. Any kind of days you like. (*Drinks quickly.*)

[FIFI *drains glass.*

FIFI. That's just exquisite, isn't it ?

ALF. Now, will you listen ?

FIFI (*picks up a rose or other flower*). Ah, how sweet ! This is for your button-hole. (*Bus. of reaching over to put it in* ALFRED'S *coat.*)

ALF. (*catching* FIFI's *hand*). You must listen, now. I have something to ask you — and you will promise not to refuse me. My happinesss depends upon it. It may be my life-long happiness. You will not refuse me when you know how much —

EVAN. (*cries out*). Oh ! (*Sinks swooning on chair back of table* R. [ALFRED *springs to his feet and looks round.*

MUSIC. — Swell for EVANGELINE ; *bus. Down again very pp. for dialogue, getting change of effect.*

ALF. (*rising*). Evangeline ! (*Hastens to her.*)

FIFI (*aside; not rising*). Ah, a little love episode ! (*Goes on with her breakfast tranquilly.*)

ALF. What a cursed coincidence !

FIFI. Yes, doctor. It was unfortunate, I admit.

ALF. Evangeline !

    [EVANGELINE *revives. Rises with difficulty.* ALFRED
      tries to assist her, but she will not permit it.

FIFI (*aside*). I'm almost sorry for the little innocent. (*Drinks champagne cheerfully.*)

    [EVANGELINE *walks slowly and weakly toward her
      door*, R. 3. ALFRED *again tries to assist her, but
      she repulses him.*

EVAN. (*bus.; weakly*). No !

ALF. Believe me, I am innocent !

FIFI (*rising from ottoman; aside*). O, yes, they are always innocent.

ALF. You are mistaken, if you think — that I — that we — (*To* FIFI.) Miss Oritanski, I beg you to tell her how it was.   [*READY* JOSEPHINE, *to enter up* R.

FIFI. My dear doctor (*wiping her fingers daintily with napkin, and tossing it down*), I would be charmed to do so — charmed (*moves backward to her door*, L. 3) ; but there's one quite serious objection — the young lady evidently saw how it was herself. (*EXIT into her room*, L. 3.)

ALF. (*realizing that* FIFI *has made matters a hundred times worse*). Good Heavens ! (*Turns to* EVANGELINE *in desperation.*) Evangeline ! You must listen, my darling.

EVAN. (*at her door*, R. 3). No — I would rather not — now —

ALF. But, my darling, you must hear me ! You must listen, Evangeline, for I can explain exactly how — how —

EVAN. Yes, of course you have excuses. But, O Alfred ! what difference could it make — what difference could anything make — when I saw (*voice full of emotion*) —the dread-

ful affair — with my own eyes ?   (*Turns, and EXIT at door*
R. 3).   [*Stop music.*

ALF.   Oh, this is a crime — this is — this is simply — oh
— (*paces back and forth once*).   I can't stand it — I — I'll go
and walk the streets. (*Starts up* R.   *Stops, listening at door.*)
Mrs. Bender !   I hear her familiar panting on the stairs.
(*Starts down* R.   *Stops.*)   I can't meet her now.   I'll walk
the streets some other time. (*Stops down* R.)   I must get
this out of the way. (*Moves the table back.*)   They'll be sure
to look for me in my room. (*Crosses* L.)   Dabney's room !
That's the thing !   [*EXIT* L. 2 *into* DABNEY'S *room.*

> DABNEY'S *voice heard in incoherent revelry as* ALFRED
> *goes in.   ENTER* JOSEPHINE, *door up* R., *with um-*
> *brella ; puts it in hat-rack up* L. C.   *Very excited,*
> *exhausted, disarranged, dusty, bedraggled, hot, and*
> *out of breath.   She looks fiercely around the room.*
> *Then drops into a chair* L. *of* R. *table.*

JOS.   No one there.   Not a sign — not a vestige of the
man — or of any one looking for him, excepting me — I was
looking for him — tramping up and down around that miserable Arch — in all the heat — and dust — and noise.   Oh,
there's something at the bottom of all this !

> [DABNEY'S *voice heard outside* L. 2 E.

What can be going on in there ?   (*Rises to go.*)

> [EVANGELINE *opens door* R. 3 *a little.*

Is that you, Evangeline ?   Come here !

> [EVANGELINE *comes on at* R. 3, *giving an anxious*
> *glance about the room.   Her eyes are red from weep-*
> *ing, and she is very pale.   Comes down* R. *of* JO-
> SEPHINE.

Why, my child — why Evangeline — what has happened ?

> [JOSEPHINE *rises and meets* EVANGELINE.

EVAN. (R. C.).   Oh, nothing! (*Wipes a tear away quickly.*)

> [*READY* BENDER, *to enter up* R.

JOS. (L. C.).   Where is Alfred ?

EVANGELINE *tries to speak. Cannot. Shakes head. Suddenly buries head on* JOSEPHINE'S *breast or shoulder.*

Something has gone wrong. You have quarrelled.

EVAN. (*shakes head negatively; raises head a little*). We have parted — forever. (*Head down again, and stifled sobs.*)

JOS. This is all foolishness. One of you is to blame. If it's Alfred, then he must apologize. If it's you — 'hem — he must apologize just the same.

EVAN. (*shaking head emphatically*). No! I never — want to see him again (*raises head*), mamma. He left me — at the Dickermans' — to look for my lost bracelet — and I found him here — breakfasting with the opera singer. Yes, and worse than breakfasting.

JOS. Worse!

EVAN. Hundreds and hundreds of times worse. He was — he was holding her hands — and telling her — that — that — Oh!

(*Breaks down and sobs on* JOSEPHINE'S *shoulder.*)

JOS. I must look into this.

EVAN. It won't — do any good — I've looked into it. That was enough.

ENTER BENDER *up* R., *rushing in hurriedly and excitedly.*

BEND. (*as he crosses down to* L.). Not at the theatre! Where the dev— Thunder and lightning — my wife! (*Down* L.)

[JOSEPHINE *leads* EVANGELINE *to door* R. 3 *in silence, and motions her to go in. EXIT* EVANGELINE R. 3. JOSEPHINE *turns and faces* BENDER.

(*Trying to command a cheerful tone.*) Ah, my angel! Been out — or just going?

JOS. (*coming back to* R. C.). I have a few words to say to you. [BENDER *looks a trifle apprehensive.* (*Taking letter from pocket and extending it toward him.*) Do you see this?

BEND. (L. C.; *rather weakly*). Oh, yes — I — I see it. (*As* JOSEPHINE *still holds it out, he takes it.*) Looks like the one you snatched up so nervously this morning.

JOS. (R. C.). It is.

BEND. (L. C.). Ah! May I — read it?

JOS. May you read it?

BEND. (*slight start*). I believe I — suggested —

JOS. (*commandingly*). Read it.

BEND. (L. C.; *quite subdued*). Yes — that was the idea that I —

[JOSEPHINE *motions him. He stops. He reads the letter calmly.*

JOS. (R. C.; *watching closely. Aside*). He does not move an eye-lash. He is innocent. [BENDER *finishes letter.* (*Aloud.*) Well?

BEND. Quite amusing, my dear. (*Hands her the letter.*) Ha, ha, ha! (*Rather a forced laugh.*)

JOS. Yes, isn't it? Ha, ha, ha! (*Rather a bitter laugh.*)

BEND. I only wish you had gone there.

JOS. I did go there.

BEND. (L.). Ha? You really went? Ha, ha, ha! Then I wish I'd gone.

JOS. (R.). What!

BEND. (*seriously*). No — that is, only to see you, my love — to see you enjoy yourself.

JOS. Oh! (*Though still frowning darkly, she is somewhat mollified. She turns and looks toward ALFRED'S door,* R. 1, *as if with a new thought. After looking sharply at BENDER.*) Theodore, do you think I do not know who wrote that letter? (*Shaking letter in hand.*)

BEND. (*blankly*). You — you don't say!

JOS. (R.). I do say — and I say that the person is not ten steps from me at this instant.

BEND. (L., *beginning to show considerable alarm, though he turns so that* JOSEPHINE *does not observe it. Aside.*) My soul!

Jos. Now, shall I tell you why this person wrote it?

Bend. (*thoroughly unnerved and aghast*). Oh — er — perhaps there's no need of going into that, my dear.

Jos. (*hotly*). There is need of going into that. He wrote it, Bender, to get me out of the way, so that he could enjoy a breakfast *tête-à-tête* here with our comic opera young woman (*pointing to* L. 3, *indignantly*).

Bend. (*aside*). There's no escape from this, but to confess and beg forgiveness. (*Aloud.*) My dear, I shall have to admit —

Jos. I don't want you to admit. I want you to act.

[Bender *stares with blank face at* Josephine.

Bend. (*after bus.*). Where would you like to have me act?

Jos. Here!

[Bender *stares again. Then gives an uncertain glance around the room.*

Bend. (*after bus., weakly*). Here?

[READY *noise ; and* Alfred *to enter* L. 2 E.

Jos. Here ; and now you must see him.

Bend. See — whom?

Jos. Stupid, stupid! Alfred, of course — who wrote this letter — got me out of the way — left Evangeline at the Dickermans', and then came here and breakfasted and flirted with this creature from the theatre. (*Walks about.*)

Bend. (L. C. ; *suddenly comprehending*). Eh! (*Looks about savagely.*) My breakfast! My — (*stamps foot in indignation, after seeing the remains of the breakfast.*)

Jos. (R. C. ; *turning quickly*). What!

Bend. (*recovering himself and coming down* L. C.). My — son-in-law, I say.

Jos. Isn't it shameful! (*Going up to* D. R. 3 E.)

Bend. (*crossing down* R.). Shameful? It's — it's beyond words.

Jos. (*at door* R. 3). Come here. Evangeline will tell you everything.

BEND. (*going up to* L. *of* JOSEPHINE). Yes, my dear. (*Aside.*) Saved for the present — but how the deuce will it end? [*Noises as before outside* L. 2. *ENTER* ALFRED L. 2.

ALF. (*turning and starting quickly toward door up* R.). Now, to get out before —

JOS. (*commandingly, to* C.). Wait !

> [ALFRED *stops and stands near* L. C. JOSEPHINE
> *motions* BENDER *to follow, and goes toward* ALFRED.

My husband has something to say to you.

> (*Indicates to* BENDER *to go on.*)

BEND. (R. *of* JOSEPHINE ; *aside; in agony*). If I abuse him, he'll betray me.

JOS. (C.). Come, come ! [ALFRED *looks away an instant.*

BEND. 'Hem ! (*Crosses to* ALFRED, *trying to assume a* *severity of attitude and expression.*) Sir —

> [ALFRED *turns to* BENDER. BENDER *instantly melts.*

(*Very meekly.*) Sir — I said — sir —

BENDER. ALFRED.

JOSEPHINE.

ALF. (L.). Well ? What is it ?

BEND. (C. ; *turning to* JOSEPHINE). He wants to know what it is.

JOS. (R.). Pooh !

BEND. (*to* ALFRED). Yes, pooh ! Now, you mustn't take offence, my boy —

JOS. (*catching* BENDER *by sleeve or shoulder*). Stop ! If you can't do better, I'll interfere.

BEND. (*aside*). Oh — that would end everything ! He'd let it all out. (*To* ALFRED.) Your — your behavior, sir, was — er —

JOS. (*to* BENDER, *spitefully*). Outrageous !

BEND. (*rather tamely*). Outrageous.

JOS. (*to* BENDER). Ungentlemanly !

BEND. Um — 'hem ! (*Turns to* JOSEPHINE.) Eh ?

JOS. (*to* BENDER). We are furious at you !

BEND. Yes, we are. (*Tamely.*) Very furious.

JOS. (*speaking directly to* ALFRED). You ought to be ashamed of yourself — engaged to one lady, and flirting and breakfasting with another.

BEND. (*with sudden animation and seriousness*). Yes — breakfasting with another — at my ex — er — 'hem ! (*Suddenly checks himself.*)

> ALFRED *puts both hands on his shoulders, and checks*
> BENDER *suddenly.* JOSEPHINE *has turned away*
> *for the instant.*

ALF. Mrs. Bender, I have flirted with no one — breakfasted with no one. I simply —

JOS. (*quickly*). What — you dare to deny it ? Mercy on us ! Perhaps you will go so far as to deny that you sent me this letter ? (*Bus. Crosses to* ALFRED.)

ALF. (L.). Letter ? I — sent ? (*Looks at* JOSEPHINE *and then at* BENDER.)

BEND. (R.; *aside.. Sits on the left corner of* R. *table*). Now is my time to die.

JOS. (C. ; *pushing letter into* ALFRED'S *hands*). Take the vile fabrication ! Take it !

ALF. (L. ; *aside*). His letter ! (*Looks at* BENDER.) Jove ! I have an idea — I'll do it ! For Evangeline's sake, I'll do it !

JOS. (C.). No wonder you are speechless !

ALF. (L.). No — I can't be expected to say much — under the circumstances.

JOS. Then you did write it ?

ALF. (*nonchalantly*). O yes.

JOS. (*almost a scream of triumph*). Ah ! (*To* BENDER.) I told you !

> [BENDER *stands an instant paralyzed.* ALFRED
> *stands with bowed head.*

(*To* BENDER.) Did you hear what he said ? He confessed it !

BEND. Confessed — that — he — ?

Jos. Yes. [BENDER *goes to* ALFRED *precipitately.* (*Thinking* BENDER *means to assault* ALFRED.) Oh! (*Catching* BENDER *by the arm.*)

BEND. (C.; *aside to* ALFRED). You jewel!

Jos. (R.; *seizing hold of* BENDER). No violence, Theodore!

BEND. (*to* JOSEPHINE). Unhand me, Josephine! This is my affair.

ALF. (L.; *quick aside to* BENDER). That's it! Play the indignant.

BEND. (C.; *violently*). So — you were the cowardly wretch who stooped to such a villainous, underhand trick as this. Fie! — (*Threateningly.*) I say — Fie!

ALF. (*aside to* BENDER). Go on. Fie some more.

Jos. (*aside*). Dear me! I'm afraid Theodore will do him some injury. I must reconcile them.

BEND. Is nothing on earth sacred to you? Neither my stainless past nor the future welfare of my innocent child? (*Advancing upon* ALFRED. *Very threateningly.*) Have you forgotten that a father's —

Jos. Theodore, you must not forget yourself!

BEND. I will forget myself! I forget everything but the vengeance that is due —

[JOSEPHINE *rushes around between the two men, with a cry of alarm.*

Jos. (*putting* BENDER *across to her* R.). No, you shall not hurt him! [*TABLEAU.*
(C.; *to* ALFRED.) Have you no excuse to offer for your conduct, Alfred? Nothing to say?

ALF. (L.). My dear Mrs. Bender, believe me, I was not taking a breakfast with the lady — I only happened to be there.

BEND. (R.; *aside*). I wish I'd happened to be there.

Jos. (C.). Well, I will try to believe what you say. Time brings all things to light.

BEND. (R.; *aside*). I hope it won't this time.

Jos. (C.).   So I will do what I can to reconcile Evangeline.   But first you must beg my husband's pardon.

ALF. (L.).   What?   O yes — of course.   (*To* BENDER.) You'll overlook it, I trust?

> [BENDER *stands stonily, partly turning his back, and folds his arms.*

Jos. (C.).   Theodore, you must forgive him.

BEND. (R.; *shakes head*).   He has wronged me too deeply.

> [JOSEPHINE, *bus. of putting* ALFRED'S *hand in* BENDER'S, *and going up to* D. R. 3 E.

Jos.   Now, make up and be friends.

> [JOSEPHINE *nods encouragingly, and EXIT into her room,* R. 3.

BEND. (*running up to* D. R. 3 E.   *Calling after* JOSEPHINE.) Don't leave me alone with him — something will happen.

> [*Bus. after short pause, of* BENDER *and* ALFRED *looking around cautiously, and then falling into each other's arms.*

(*Effusively.   Feelingly.   Wringing* ALFRED'S *hands.*)   My dear boy, I am overwhelmed with gratitude!

> [*READY* JOSEPHINE *and* EVANGELINE, *to enter* R. 3 E.

ALF. (L. C., *drily*).   Well, by Jove, you ought to be!   She'd have torn you limb from limb.

BEND. (R. C.).   Is there anything I can do for you in return?

ALF.   Certainly.   That's the precise reason I've done all this.   You must do something in return.

BEND. (R.).   What is it?

ALF. (L.).   Move out of the house with your family this very day.

BEND.   What?   Move — move out?

ALF.   And not only that, but you must persuade the opera singer to go.   She's paid her rent, so I can't do anything.   But you can.

BEND.   You're mad, my boy!

ALF. (L.).   Not in the least — but I will be if you don't go.

BEND. (R.).   But how am I to —

ENTER JOSEPHINE *with* EVANGELINE, R. 3.

JOSEPHINE.   Here she is, Alfred, ready to make peace with you.

[EVANGELINE, *with eyes downcast, down* R. C.   AL-
FRED *crosses to* EVANGELINE.   BENDER *joins* JOSE-
PHINE *up* L. C.

ALF. (*going to* EVANGELINE).   Evangeline, I hope your mother has convinced you that there was a mistake.

EVAN.   I knew there was a mistake — of some kind. (EVANGELINE, *after a short struggle with herself, gives* ALFRED *her hand.*)   I will try to forget it, Alfred, but I could not remain in the house — it would be impossible while that dreadful person is permitted to live here.

ALF. *and* BEND.   What!   (*They exchange glances.*)

EVAN.   Oh, yes, she must go away!   Papa will have to see that she does it.   And until then we will take rooms at the hotel near the corner of Southgate Street.   It isn't far, you know.

ALF. (*aside*).   By Jove — if this isn't luck!

EVAN. (*crosses to* ALFRED *and goes up* C.).   Mamma and I have arranged it all — and I'm going over there now to engage the rooms.   Perhaps — perhaps you would like to come with me.

ALF. (*going up to* EVANGELINE).   I shall be delighted. (*Goes up* R. *to* EVANGELINE.)   Ah, Evangeline!   (*Near door; gets hold of her hand.*)   You must believe me innocent of any —

EVAN. (*finger to lips*).   Sh!   (*Points to* FIFI'S *room.*)

ALF.   Oh, the deuce!

[*EXEUNT* EVANGELINE *and* ALFRED, *door up* R.

JOS. (*down* R. C.).   Well — you see what must be done.   I could not pacify Evangeline in any other way.   The woman must be got rid of.

BEND. (*down* L. C.).   But it can't be done, my dear -- she's paid in advance.   .

      [JOSEPHINE *makes a slight start.   She gives* BENDER
        a quick look. BENDER *starts.   Looks alarmed.*

JOS. (*sternly*).   How do you know that ?

BEND.   The fact is, Josephine, Alfred himself just spoke to me about getting her to leave.   He asked me to — to help him arrange it.

JOS.   Oh, he did !   (*Thinks.*)   Then we must do it.

BEND.   All very well to say — but how ?   That's the question.

JOS.   If I only had some excuse, I could very soon make her pack up.

BEND.   Oh, yes.   If you had some excuse.   (*Slight sneer.*)

JOS. (*with sudden idea*).   Ah !   (*Nods her head as if it would do.*)   Theodore, you shall furnish me one.

BEND.   I ?   How can I —

JOS.   By making love to her.

BEND. (*in an injured tone*).   Oh, my dear !

JOS.   No nonsense, now !   It is just the thing, and we will do it at once.   (*Glances around as if surveying the room.*) You must meet her here — in this room — alone.   You must be very attentive — in fact, affectionate.

BEND. (L. C.).   Heavens, Josephine, what do you — !

JOS. (R. C.).   Sh !   You can do it.   In the meantime I will use that small ladder and observe the whole affair from the transom there, over our door.   (*Points to* D. R. 3 E.)

BEND. (*aside ; alarmed*).   My soul !

                [*READY* FIFI, *to enter* L. 3 E.

JOS.   At the proper time — just when it has gone far enough —I will scream, rush in, and make such a scene that the creature will be glad to escape with her life.

BEND. (*aside*).   I'll be glad to escape with mine.

JOS. (*going, taking the hamper off ottoman, and placing it on chair,* R., *between the doors*).   This will work beautifully.

BEND. (*crosses down* R.; *aside*). Great Cæsar! The opera singer will betray me.

JOS. (*up* L. *Bus.*). I read of just such a case in a book, and it worked beautifully. (JOSEPHINE *knocks at* FIFI'S *door*, L. 3.)

BEND. (R., *to* JOSEPHINE). Hold on — what — what are you doing?

JOS. (*hurrying across to* R. 3 E.). You have simply to do as I told you — leave the rest to me.

(*EXIT* R. 3, *shutting the door after her carefully.*)

BEND. (*going up and down* C.). Heavens and earth and — and the other place — I'm in for it now!

[JOSEPHINE *appears at the transom over door* R. 3, *opening it.*

JOS. (*at transom*). Now, be careful.

BEND. (C., *with deep meaning*). I will.

ENTER FIFI *from her room*, L. 3.

FIFI (*looking from door* L. 3 E., *inquiringly*). Did any one knock? (*She sees* BENDER. *Speaks very sweetly.*) Oh, Mr. Bender, are you there? (*Coming down slowly in front of ottoman.*)

BEND. (C.). Yes, I'm here. (*A glance of misery to* R.) I thought — perhaps — you'd join in a little — er — chat —

FIFI (L.). A chat? Oh, certainly. Nothing could be more charming. (*Aside.*) How awkward the man is.

(FIFI *sits* L. C. *on ottoman, facing to* L.)

BEND. (*going round at back of ottoman, to* L. *Seating himself* L. *of* FIFI). Now, if she'll only keep quiet about the breakfast — and the dressmaker's bill!

Ottoman.

| FIFI. | BENDER. |

FIFI (*laughs out merrily*). Why, Mr. Bender, what is the matter with you to-day? You don't seem like the same man I — [*READY* McSNATH, *to enter up* R.

BEND. (*quickly*). 'Hem — 'hem — (*coughs to cover up her*

remark).   Oh, nothing, my dear !   I dare say you've heard me going about whistling and — and — carolling with joy ; but you know we have different moods.

FIFI.   Perhaps you have had a little matrimonial scene with Mrs. Bender, eh ?

BEND.   No — no — impossible l   We are like turtle doves.

FIFI.   Dear me !   I didn't know that turtle doves suffered so much.   (*Laughs lightly.*)

JOS. (*aside*).   Oh, the little fiend !

FIFI (*archly*).   What do you think the other turtle dove would say if she saw this turtle dove sitting here with me ?

BEND. (*confused.*)   Ahem — I —

> [JOSEPHINE *motions him to go on.*   BENDER *nods to his wife, and suddenly takes* FIFI'S *hand.*

Ah, my dear young lady —

FIFI (*smiling*).   There — now you're more like yourself again.

BEND. (*jumping half up, and trying to cover up* FIFI'S *remark*).   Ah, 'hem — yes — as you say — the — er — weather is more like itself again.   (*He still has her hand.*)

> *ENTER* AUGUSTUS MCSNATH *abruptly, door up* R. *He stops* R., *and stands looking at* BENDER.   JOSE-PHINE *begins to motion to* BENDER *violently, from the transom.*   BENDER *finally sees her, and looks up* R.   *Seeing* MCSNATH, *he instantly drops* FIFI'S *hand, and starts back.*   FIFI *looks around and sees* MCSNATH, *but is perfectly composed.*

FIFI.   Ah, we have an audience.

MCSNATH (*to* C.; *stops on seeing the situation*).   Beg pardon, my name is McSnath.

BEND. (L.).   Is it ?

MCSN. (C.; *suspiciously looking at* BENDER).   It is — I said it was.

BEND.   Well, I didn't say it wasn't.

FIFI.   OTTOMAN.   BENDER.
            McSNATH.

McSn.   I didn't say you did.   [*Pause.*

Jos. (*motioning to* BENDER. *Loud whisper. Aside to him*).
Get him away — get him away.

McSn.   I'm an old friend of Mr. Pettibone. We haven't
met for years.

BEND.   Don't say?

McSn.   I do say. I said we hadn't met —

BEND.   I heard you.

McSn.   Is he at home?

BEND.   No.

McSn.   I'm sorry.

BEND.   So am I.

McSn.   Stayed over a day, just to see my dear old Pettibone.

BEND.   Well, there's no such a person as your dear old
Pettibone here.   [McSNATH *looks suspiciously at* BENDER.

McSn. (*aside*).   Something out of the way going on. Very
suspicious looking — I'll hunt him up, and tell him about it.
He ought to know.   [*READY noise of falling step-ladder.*

BEND.   Good-day, sir.

McSn.   I'll call again.

BEND.   We shall enjoy a visit from you at any time.

> [McSNATH *goes up* R. *Turns at door and looks back.*
> BENDER *keeps his eye on* McSNATH. *EXIT* Mc-
> SNATH, *door up* R.

(*Takes* FIFI's *hand passionately.*) Thank Heaven, he's gone!
You dear little — (*starts back; aside*). Oh, Lord! I forgot
my wife. (*Sinks on seat beside* FIFI.)

Jos. (*aside*).   He's doing splendidly now.

FIFI.   Oh, Mr. Bender, you must excuse me for not waiting breakfast for —   [*READY* ALFRED *to enter up* R.

BEND. (*bus.; sudden endeavor to interrupt*). Ah, ahem!
(*At the same time seizing a book from table or chair near at*

hand, and throwing it on floor.)   Yes.   (*Seizes her hand.*)
No words can express it.   [FIFI *stares in surprise.*

Jos. (*aside*).   What is the matter with the man?

FIFI.   And after you had been so good about the dress-maker's little —

BEND. (*bus. as before, only still more excited.   This time, he sends a vase crashing to the floor.   Rises, and exclaims in a loud voice, to drown* FIFI'S *remarks*).   Oh — ah — yes — my dear!   Have you ever seen this album — ahem?   (*Bus. seizing a portfolio from desk,* L., *throwing several books down, and opening it suddenly before* FIFI.   BENDER *stands trembling, and wipes perspiration from his brow.*)

FIFI (*aside*).   I wonder if he's been drinking!   (*She glances at the book which* BENDER *shoved before her.   Aloud.*)
Why, that isn't an album, Mr. Bender!

         [*READY* TOM *and* EVANGELINE, *to enter up* R.

BEND.   Eh?   (*Snatches it away.*)   Oh!   (*Aside.*)   This is killing me.   The only way is to plunge in, and bring matters to a climax.   (*Aloud; sinking and kneeling beside* FIFI, *and putting his arm around her.*)   Miss Oritanski — I cannot conceal the beating of my heart — I cannot hide from you the fact, guilty though it is, that I love —

         MUSIC, comedy dramatic music with element of con-fusion and hurry in it.   Play pp. for dialogue.

         ENTER ALFRED *up* R. *hastily, anticipating cue a little.   He stops an instant in astonishment,* C.
         BENDER *sees* ALFRED, *and signs to him frantically to go away.*

ALF. (C.; *coming into room quickly*).   Look here, Bender, you must be crazy!   I can't get you out of another scrape as I did with that confounded letter of yours, by taking it on myself —

         [BENDER *jumps up with shout of alarm.*   JOSEPHINE
         utters a ghastly shriek, and disappears from tran-som R. 3.   *Sound outside* R. 3, *of crash, bang, and*

clatter of falling step-ladder; and at same time door
R. 3 *opens, and* JOSEPHINE *falls swooning into the*
room C., *with ladder fallen partly in door near her.*
FIFI *screams and runs to her door* L. 3 *where she*
stands frightened.

FIFI (L. 3 E.).   His wife!

   [TOM *rushes on at door up* R. EVANGELINE *runs on*
   at door up R. *and falls on her knees by* JOSEPHINE,
   with exclamation of alarm. *READY curtain.*

EVAN. (R. C.; *bus.*).   Oh, what is it, mamma?

TOM *up* C.

ALFRED.   FIFI.

EVANGELINE.   JOSEPHINE, on stage.

Ottoman.

BENDER.

ALF.   Good Heavens, what have I done!

BEND.   You've wrecked the entire family.

TOM. (*up* C.).   Ge-Whiffles!   Now, he'll get all the comforts of home.

MUSIC.   Forte for curtain.   Stop on curtain down.
RING curtain.

CURTAIN.

ACT IV.

SCENE. Same as in Act I. BENDER *is discovered up* R., *sitting on the bottom stair, with his head buried in his hands as if in mental agony, and in such a way that he does not at first attract attention. READY* ALFRED *and* EVANGELINE, *to enter* R. 3 E.

BEND.   It was kind of Alfred and Evangeline to intercede for me — but — (*shaking head*) — no use — no use. (*Turns up sadly. Speaks meditatively, in a low voice.*)   My wife — was never in such a state — before — never.

> *ENTER* ALFRED *and* EVANGELINE R. 3, *with a subdued quietness as if a dead body lay in the room. They close the door quietly and carefully.* BENDER *turns to them, looking for a gleam of hope.*

(*Low voice.*)   Well ?

> [*All come forward. READY* JOSEPHINE, *to enter* R. 3 E.

ALF. (C.; *shakes head*).   She won't listen to anything.

EVAN. (R.).   We reasoned with her all we could, papa.

> [BENDER L.

EVAN. (R.).   She is going to move to the hotel, and has already ordered the trunks taken over.   She — she is to meet a lawyer there at four o'clock.

BEND. (L.).   A lawyer?

> [EVANGELINE *and* ALFRED *nod sadly.*

ALF. (C.).   Yes — Tom has gone out to bring one.

BEND.   And — what did she say — about me ?

EVAN. *and* ALF.   Nothing.

> [BENDER *repeats "nothing" with his lips alone — no sound. He looks at* ALFRED. ALFRED *shakes his head.*

EVAN. Oh papa — if a divorce could be avoided! (*She puts her head down on* ALFRED'S *shoulder to hide her tears.*)

BEND. (*after pause*). And — you really think she would be so cruel — so heartless as to — !

> *MUSIC. A sweet, sad strain, pp. " con expressione."*
> *Play a few bars for* JOSEPHINE'S *entrance; then stop.*
>
> *ENTER* JOSEPHINE R. 3. BENDER, *seeing* JOSE-
> PHINE, *breaks off with "Ahem" and a cough, and*
> *looks wanderingly toward other parts of the room.*

JOS. (*down between* ALFRED *and* BENDER). I am glad, children, that you are alone, for I have something to say.

> [BENDER *turns slowly and looks at* JOSEPHINE *in*
> *ghastly astonishment.* ALFRED *looks at* JOSEPHINE
> *in surprise also.*

EVAN. (*crosses to* JOSEPHINE). But, mamma dear — we're not alone.

JOS. (L. C.). Indeed! (*Looks about room.*) I fail to see any one else.

BEND. (L. *aside*). I must be growing thin.

JOS. I wished to inform you that I have decided not to go home, but to find some quiet watering-place where no prying eyes will intrude upon my widow's sorrow.

BEND. (*suddenly breaking out*). Oh, look here! This is going a little — a — a —

> [JOSEPHINE *looks sternly and coldly at* BENDER, *freez-*
> *ing him into silence.* BENDER *is frozen. Bus.*

JOS. (L. C.; *turning to* EVANGELINE). It is singular that a stranger should have the audacity to address us.

EVAN. (R. C.). A stranger, mamma?

JOS. I said a stranger. (*Darts an indignant glance at* BENDER. BENDER *quails,* L.) You will of course come with me, Evangeline, and you, Alfred, must join us as soon as you can. Then the whole family will be united again.

ALF. (R.; *rather timidly*). And — and your husband — ?

Jos. My husband — my — ? (*Stops and stands as if holding back tears.*) We will sometimes think of him. He was a man who had some good qualities.

Evan. (*with new hope; eagerly*). Yes, mamma.

Jos. But they were few and far between.

Bend. (*forgetting himself again*). Josephine, you'll do me the credit of —

> [*Bus. of glance as before, stopping* Bender *in the midst of his line.* Bender *again frozen.*

Jos. I wish to do justice to the memory of one who has passed away.

Bend. (*aside*). Thunder and lightning! This is not pleasant at all. (*Walks about and down on the* L.)

Jos. I wish this person wouldn't disturb us. (*Going to* D. R. 3 E. *After looking at* Bender *an instant, turns to* Evangeline.) Evangeline, my child, you had better go over to our rooms at the hotel for the present. I will come soon. (*Crosses to door.*)

Evan. (C.). Yes, mamma.

> [Bender *stops pacing and looks at them.* Evangeline *looks uncertainly at* Bender. *Slight pause.*

Jos. (*up* R.; *to* Evangeline. *Speaks with a cold, calm voice.*) Children, if you desire to take leave of your former father, I have no objection. (*Goes slowly off* R. 3.)

> [*Slight pause. All three draw long breaths.*

Bend. (L.). There goes my widow.

Alf. (*crosses to* Bender, L. *Sympathetically.*) Yes (*taking* Bender's *hand and pressing it*), so far as I see, you're a dead man. (*Crosses back to* R.)

> [*READY* Mrs. Pettibone *and* Emily, *to enter up* R.

Bend. (*to* Evangeline). Evangeline (Evangeline *to the* R. *of* Bender), you received permission to take a last look at the remains. (*Holds out hand to* Evangeline.)

Evan. (R. C.; *going quickly to* Bender *and embracing him*). Oh, papa, I am so sorry!

BEND. (L. C.). Thank you! Thank you!

EVAN. (*looks round to* R. 3; *then more confidentially*). You shall come with me to the hotel, and we will try to think of some way to appease her. (*Urges* BENDER *up* R.)

> [BENDER *goes up* R. *with* EVANGELINE. ALFRED *crosses to* L.

BEND. (*up* R.; *turning at door up* R.). Alfred, my boy, let me know when I am to be buried.

EVAN. (*up* R. *Shocked. As they go off*). Oh!

> [*EXEUNT* EVANGELINE *and* BENDER, *door up* R.

ALF. (L.; *sits on ottoman; laughs a little.*) Poor papa Bender! Heaven only knows how he'll get out of this scrape. But I've got my own affairs to get out of — I can't be expected to worry about his. Thank the Lord, the house is nearly empty — and yet — that telegram! It gives me the cold shivers when I think of it. Oh, nonsense! They'd be here before this if they were coming. I dare say they got my dispatch. That ought to stop them.

> [*He starts toward door up* R. *Seeing* MRS. PETTI-
> BONE *and* EMILY *enter, he drops down* R., *and sits
> in chair* L. *of* R. *table. ENTER door up* R., MRS.
> PETTIBONE *and* EMILY, *in travelling rig, carrying
> satchels, parcels, etc. They come in very abruptly,
> and see* ALFRED *at once. They put down satchels,
> etc., up* C. *on table.*

MRS. P. Ah, Alfred! (*She goes down to* ALFRED, *and crosses to* L.)

EMILY. Is that — ? (*She goes to* R. *of* ALFRED.) Why, so it is!

MRS. P. Yes, here he is — as large as life.

> [*Bus. of* MRS. PETTIBONE *and* EMILY *shaking his
> hands.* ALFRED'S *arms hang limp.*

EMILY (C.). Goodness! What's the matter with him? He must be asleep. Here! Wake up! (*She shakes him.*)

> [ALFRED *recovers himself*, R. C.

ALF. Oh — yes — how-dy'-do ?   Glad to see you.

EMILY (*going up* C.).   Well, it's about time !

MRS. P. (L.).   You received our telegram, of course ?

ALF. (R. C.; *quickly*).   Yes — but you didn't get mine ?

EMILY (*up* C.).   Yours ?   No.

ALF.   And I sent it "collect."

MRS. P.   What did you say in it ?

ALF.   I told you not to — oh — well — it's of no conse-
quence now, you know.

EMILY (*up* C.).   You told us — not to — ?

ALF.   Not to — er — delay a moment. (*Aside.*)   Hang
it, I hate to lie like that !

[EMILY *up* C. ; MRS. PETTIBONE L.

EMILY ⎫
MRS. P. ⎭ (*relieved*).   Oh !

MRS. P.   And, now, Alfred, it is best for you to know at
once why we are here, without my husband's knowledge, for
it concerns you and Emily very deeply — very deeply.

[ALFRED *looks at ladies anxiously*.

EMILY (*coming down* C.).   Oh, mamma, dear, you're making such a tragic affair out of it !

MRS. P. (L. ; *cuttingly*).   Indeed ! Perhaps you can break
the intelligence with more levity ?

EMILY (C.; *going to* ALFRED *on his* L.; *laughing*).   I'm
sure there's no breaking about it. You see, Alfred — cousin
Alfred (*laughs*), you and I have been about half or three-
quarters engaged to each other for some time. Now, although
we're very fond of each other — aren't we ? — still, we both
know it isn't exactly the kind required.

[ALFRED *says nothing*.

I know you do — and I know I do — so, don't you think it is
about time the engagement was — 'hem — (*burlesque comedy
gesture*) frustrated ?

ALF. (R. C. ; *rising; suddenly seizing* EMILY's *hand*).   You
don't mean it !

EMILY (C. ; *laughing ; turning to* MRS. PETTIBONE). See that ? What did I tell you ! The boy is so delighted, he hasn't the politeness to conceal it.

ALF. Oh, no !

EMILY. Oh, yes ! And I really believe (*an idea coming to her. Slowly raises her finger and points it at him*) — Alfred ! You have been falling in love, too !

ALF. Too !

EMILY (*catching herself*). Oh ! (*Hand over mouth an instant.*) [*READY* DABNEY, *to enter* L. 2 E.

ALF. Then you — then she — ha, ha, ha ! (*Looks from one to the other. Both nod their heads affirmatively.*) Really ! Ha, ha ! Bless you ! I congratulate you. (*Seizing* EMILY'S *hand, and then, in his enthusiasm,* MRS. PETTIBONE'S *also.*) I — I — oh, this is joyful ! ha, ha, ha ! (*Falling in chair* L. *of* R. *table.*)

EMILY (C.). Well — upon my word ! (*Going up* C., *piqued.*)

ALF. Who is the unfortunate man ? (*Rises.*)

EMILY *and* MRS. P. (*together*). What !

ALF. No, fortunate, of course — ha, ha, ha ! We must be friends. I'll treat him royally — a drive — down the Strand — o' na'bus — Aquarium — (*etc., for London local gags*). Why don't you tell me his name ? (*Up to* EMILY.)

[MRS. PETTIBONE *and* EMILY *have been in vain trying to stop the flow of* ALFRED'S *enthusiasm.*)

MRS. P. *and* EMILY. Victor Smythe.

ALF. Ha — Vic — (*aside*). By George !

MRS. P. (*up to* EMILY *and* ALFRED). Yes ; he has been devoted to Emily for a long time ; but for some reason, your uncle seems to have a particular aversion to the young man.

ALF. (*meaningly*). Yes — he has.

MRS. P. I have done all I could to smooth matters over.

[ALFRED *smothers a laugh.* ENTER DABNEY

from his room, L. 2, *towel around his head, nursing his head still, and in evident misery.*

Why, who is that person?

EMILY (*seeing* DABNEY). Dear me!

ALF. That — ah — yes! You mean — oh! That? (*Speaks confidentially.*) Poor fellow, he has seen better days. A victim of cruel misfortune — drunken wife — starving children — and all that. I took pity on him. He helps me, 'hem — keep the house in order. (*Aside.*) That's true.

[DABNEY *sinks on ottoman,* L. C.

MRS. P. (*pityingly*). How sad the poor fellow seems.

EMILY. Yes — but come, mamma; it would hardly do to have Mr. Smythe find us looking like this.

ALF. Smythe! He isn't coming here!

MRS. P. Yes — we sent word to him from the station.

[ALFRED *gives a look of resignation.* DABNEY *catches sight of the ladies, and rises quickly, hurriedly trying to arrange his collar and conceal the towel he had against his head.*

DAB. (*rises to* L. C.). I most humbly crave pardon. I was not aware there were ladies present.

MRS. P. (*going to* DABNEY). Ah — do not speak of it, dear sir. We know all. (*Goes up.*)

[DABNEY *astonished.* ALFRED *picks up book or paper, and watches bus. over the top of it.*

EMILY (*down to* R. *of* DABNEY). Yes — and you mustn't be down-hearted. Things will be better by-and-by. (*Goes up.*)

DAB. (*involuntary motion toward head*). I hope so, I'm sure.

MRS. P. (*down* R. *of* DABNEY. *Suddenly putting money into* DABNEY'S *hand.*) Pray accept that. Only a trifle, but it may relieve you. (*She quickly goes up to door* L. 3, *and EXIT.*)

[DABNEY, *overcome with surprise, turns and watches her off.   READY* PETTIBONE, *to enter up* R.

EMILY (*down* R. *of* DABNEY. *Impulsively. Same bus. of giving* DABNEY *money*). For your starving little ones. (*Goes quickly up to door* L. 3, *and EXIT.*)

> ALFRED *sits* L. *of* R. *table.* DABNEY, *bus. of amazement. He watches* EMILY *off* L. 3 E. DABNEY *goes to* ALFRED *in a state of blank astonishment.* ALFRED *has picked up book or paper, which he pretends to be reading as he stands up* R. C.

DAB. (*looking at money in his hands*). What does all this mean?

ALF. (*looking up from book*). All what, mean?

DAB. (L. C.). Why did they give me money for my starving children?

ALF. (R. C.). Who?

DAB. Those ladies.

ALF. (*looking around room*). What ladies?

DAB. (L. C.). Who were here a moment ago.

ALF. (*shakes head*). Haven't been any ladies here. (*Resumes perusal of book.*)

DAB. Ha! (*Bus. Rubs eyes. Feels head. Looks at money.*) Perhaps I'd better go out and get some air.

ALF. Yes, do. (*Moves down near chair,* R.)

> [DABNEY *goes up* R. *Just as he gets near stairway, the door up* R. *opens, and he stands back a little.*
> *ENTER* MR. PETTIBONE, *door up* R. *hurriedly. He sees* ALFRED *at once.*

PET. Ugh! Alfred! (*He is evidently laboring under great excitement. Mechanically tosses his umbrella, rugs, etc., to* DABNEY, *without looking at him, and comes down* R. C.)

> [DABNEY *catches the articles thrown to him, and stands an instant in still deeper and blanker bewilderment. Puts hand to head. Blinks. Then turns and EXIT door up* R., *carrying the luggage in his arms.*

ALF. (*aside*). Merciful powers! (*Drops into chair.*)

PET. (L.; *going up and putting hat and coat on hat rack*). You didn't expect to see me, I dare say.

ALF. (R.; *face indicating that this is the end of everything*). O yes — I thought you'd come.

> [PETTIBONE, *coming down, shakes* ALFRED'S *hand very hurriedly, and without show of feeling.* AL-FRED *rises meekly for bus. of shaking hands.*

PET. (L. C.). I came here to sell this house.

> [*READY* EMILY *and* MRS. PETTIBONE, *to enter* L. 3 E.

ALF. (R. C.; *gasp*). Sell it!

PET. Yes — sell it — sell it. I will never live in the neighborhood. What do you think? Letters have come to her — while we were away. I am going to dispose of everything I own — everything — and then take her to America — or some other half-civilized country. I'll see you again in a moment — I must draw up some papers regarding the sale, and put them in the hands of my attorney. (*Goes toward* L.)

ALF. Yes — of course. Ahem! Where did you leave the family?

PET. The family? Don't ask — no matter. (*Goes* L. *Turns again.*) Venice — I believe it was. I told them I was going to Hamburg on business. That was a lie. (*EXIT* L. 2.)

ALF. (*sits on ottoman* L.; *aside*). This is the finishing stroke. It doesn't make any difference what happens now. Things have gone beyond me — but there's (*rises*) Emily and

> [*READY knock up* R.

Auntie. I'll warn them. (*Goes to door* L. 3.) It may do some good yet. (*Knocks on door* L. 3. *Speaks in low voice.*) Say — you two — come out, quick. *To* C.).

> *ENTER* EMILY *and* MRS. PETTIBONE L. 3. AL-FRED *signs them to be quiet.* EMILY *comes down* R. *of* ALFRED. MRS. PETTIBONE L.

EMILY *and* MRS. P. What's the matter, Alfred?

ALF. (C.).   Sh — Uncle's here!

EMILY *and* MRS. P.   What!

> [*READY* McSNATH, *to enter up* R.

ALF.   Just arrived.   Going to sell the house.   Fact is, the reason he has been going on so lately is that he thinks this Smythe chap has been paying attentions to you (*indicating* MRS. PETTIBONE).

MRS. P. (L.).   Me!   ME!   [*Both ladies surprised.*

EMILY (R.; *indignantly*).   The idea!

MRS. P.   Emily, I have said all along that this concealment was perfectly absurd.   Now I shall have a talk with Mr. Pettibone.   Alfred, do hurry to Mr. Smythe's lodgings, 251 Wells Court Road, and tell him not to come here on any account, until I send him word.

ALF.   Very well.   (*Goes up* R.   *Turns to them.*)   Lock yourself in that room — don't stir until I get back.   (*EXIT, door up* R.)   [*Door of* L. 2 *opens.*

EMILY (*seeing door* L. 2 *open*).   Oh — it's papa!

MRS. P.   Hurry!

> [MRS. PETTIBONE *and* EMILY *run hastily into room* L. 3, *and close and lock the door.*
>
> *ENTER* PETTIBONE, *door* L. 2, *with papers, etc., and plasters.*

PET.   Alfred!   (*Looks about; sees that* ALFRED *is not there.*)   What has the boy been doing?   I never saw such horrible confusion in my life.   Everything upside down. Full of medicine-bottles, plasters, music-scores — (*throwing plasters off* L. 2 E.; *going* R.).   I can't do any work there. (*Crosses to* R.)   [*A knock on door up* R. (PETTIBONE *stops.*)   Who is it?

> *ENTER* McSNATH, *door up* R., *comes down* L. C.

McS. (L. C.).   Ah!   My dear Pettibone!   I'm glad to find you at last.   (McSNATH *comes down to* PETTIBONE *and stops.*)

PET. (R. C.).   Find me?   What do you — who are you?

McS. Why, McSnath — your ancient friend McSnath. You haven't forgotten? (*Holds out hand.*)

Pet. (*shaking* McSnath's *hand mechanically, and dropping it at once.*) Oh, McSnath. Ancient friend. Yes. Glad to see you — sit down. (*Goes* R., *absently.*)

[McSnath *astonished. Follows* Pettibone *with eyes.*

McS. (*sits* L. *of* R. *table; aside*). Odd sort of welcome this is, I must say. Something's wrong with him. (*Aloud.*) You've been out of town, I believe?

Pet. (*extreme* R.). Eh? Oh — yes — yes — I believe so.

McS. I called here only a short time ago.

Pet. Yes — I dare say you did.

McS. I did. That's what I say. And although I didn't find you at home, I had the pleasure of seeing your wife.

Pet. (*suddenly aroused. Turns*). Eh!

McS. (*aside*). Ah! That's what is troubling him. (*Rises and crosses to* L.)

Pet. (R. C.). You say you saw — ?

McS. (L. C.). My dear friend — calm yourself; but take my advice and don't go off on a journey again.

Pet. What are you talking about?

McS. Now, be calm, I say! No wonder her behavior enrages you.

Pet. Ah! (*Quick exclamation.*) How do you know that?

McS. Good Heavens! Couldn't I see?

Pet. See what?

McS. What was going on a couple of hours ago — in this room. Your wife seated there — enjoying the society of a gentleman, and, from all appearances, enjoying it very much.

Pet. (*half choking in effort to stop* McSnath). Aw — gig — stop! Nonsense! Absurd! I left my wife in Venice — day before yesterday. Venice! Do you hear? (Petti- bone *walks about savagely.*)

[*READY knock, and* SMYTHE *to enter up* R.

McS. (*glances about room, having gone up to luggage on table up* C.) Oh, you did ! (McSNATH *moves about slowly.*)

PET. (*up* R. C.). Yes, I did.

McS. (*up* L. C., *picking up shawls or satchels up* C.). Whose are these ?

[PETTIBONE *turns and looks. Rushes up and seizes luggage, looking wildly at it.*

PET. (*screams, dropping things on table*). Ah — !

McS. Venice, I think you said ?

PET. (*choking with rage*). What does — who — ah — where — Oh — I'll sift this thing to the bottom now ! (*Walks about excitedly.*) The bottom ! The bottom !

McS. That's right. The bottom.

PET. (*suddenly seizes* McSNATH'S *hand*). Old friend — you will stand by me ? Say you will.

McS. I will.

NOTE. *Play very rapidly from here to end of the act. They wring each other's hands. A knock at door up* R., *both looking up suspiciously.*

PET. Come in !

ENTER VICTOR SMYTHE *door up* R. *He comes into room inquiringly.*

SMYTHE (R. C.). I beg pardon —

PET. (C.; *yell*). Ah ! (*Rushes toward* SMYTHE, *who retreats to* R. *of* R. *table.*) There he is ! By what right do you enter this house ? Answer, before I strangle you where you stand !

SMYTHE. Really, sir — I — I came in response to a request from a — lady.

PET. Say it ! Say it, sir ! From my wife !

SMYTHE. It was the lady I once supposed to be your wife —

PET. Ah ! (*As if faint.*) A chair !

[McSNATH *assists him to ottoman.*

SMYTHE (R.). I'm really very sorry, sir. I had no idea it would affect you so painfully, considering that you never were married to her —

PET. (*springing up to* C. *Bus.*) What do you mean? Never mar — Who the devil told you that?

SMYTHE (R.). T'was your servant who gave me the distressing information.   [*READY* BENDER, *to enter up* R.

PET. Servant! (*Stamps about up and down* R.) Which servant? The scoundrel! It's the most scandalous falsehood ever breathed.

SMYTHE. Falsehood? Falsehood? Oh, sir, this makes me very happy.

PET. (C.; *coming and facing* SMYTHE). Oh, sir! It doesn't make me happy at all. (*Stamps about.*) I'll — I'll get a divorce — a divorce, do you hear? — and then you can marry the woman, for all I care.

SMYTHE (*alarmed*). I — ?

PET. You! You! You! As you've been paying her such infernally devoted attentions —

McS. (L.; *aside to* PETTIBONE; *interrupting quickly*). No, no! That wasn't the one.

PET. Not the one?

McS. No. It was another man.

PET. What! Is there another? My soul! (*Walks about more excited than ever.*)

> [SMYTHE *goes up in time to be behind* D. *up* R. *as* BENDER *enters and squeezes him between door and wall.* SMYTHE, *during the following scene, stares and blinks in bewilderment, and is mainly occupied in trying to keep out of the way of others who rush about in excitement. He backs timidly from one place to another, gets behind chairs, etc.*

Why doesn't he come, so that I can kill him? Why —

> *ENTER* BENDER, *door up* R.

McS. (L.; *seeing* BENDER). There! There he is! That is the one!

PET. (L. C.). Ha! That?

[McSnath *nods.* PETTIBONE *rushes at* BENDER *as he comes down* R. C. *They meet up* R. C.

So, sir! You are here!

BEND. (C.). I seem to be. What of it?

PET. (L. C.). This of it! I want your life! I'll have satisfaction out of you! Satisfaction — you hear?

BEND. What for?

PET. I am the husband of the lady you have made love to. Now, do you understand?

BEND. You have made a mistake — my name is Bender.

PET. You'd better change it to Breaker. This good friend of mine came in here this morning, and saw you sitting there by her side.   [*READY* ALFRED, *to enter up* R.

BEND. (*aside*). Thunder and lightning!

PET. Now, sir! I shall call you to account, sir!

BEND. I'm happy to hear it, sir. And while we talk of accounts, since you are the lady's husband, you can pay this little dressmaker's bill for your wife. (*Pulls out bill.*)

PET. (*in high whining key*). What — my wife — has allowed you to pay her debts? (*Paces floor in agony.*)

BEND. (*shoving bill into* PETTIBONE'S *hand*). There's the receipt — can't you read?   [PETTIBONE *seizes the bill.*

PET. (L. C.). Ha, ha, ha! A pretty game! It says (*beating finger on bill excitedly*) Fifi Oritanski. My wife's name is Pettibone.

BEND. (R. C.). It doesn't matter — she's probably called herself that, as Pettibone was such a d——d ugly name.

PET. (*in high rage*). Ha! (*Paces about.*)

[BENDER *paces about excitedly also.*

I'll have no more words!

[*READY* MRS. PETTIBONE, *to enter* L. 3 E.

BEND. Neither will I!   [*Bus. of both threatening, etc.*

NOTE. — *Use great care to avoid carrying this scene to burlesque. It must be kept entirely natural, and played without exaggeration.*

ENTER ALFRED, *hurrying in door up* R.   SMYTHE,
on ALFRED'S *entrance, runs with fright up the stair-
case, and returns in a moment to up* C.

ALF. (*coming down*).   Smythe wasn't — (*Sees* PETTIBONE,
BENDER, *etc., and turns at once, going toward door up* R.)

PET. (*rushing and catching* ALFRED).   Here — here —
stop ! (*Brings* ALFRED *down*.)   I demand an explanation.
An explanation.   [BENDER *sits* L. *of* R. *table*.
My wife — my wife is here.

ALF. (R. C.).   You've seen her, then !

     [PETTIBONE, L. C. ; McSNATH, L. ; BENDER, R., *seated*.

PET. ⎫
McSN. ⎬ (*a subdued exclamation together*).   Ah !
BEND. ⎭

                    [McSNATH *crosses up behind to up* C.

ALF. (*going to door* L. 3, *knocks*).   Come out, auntie — he
knows you're here.

     [PETTIBONE *takes the* C.   *Sound of unlocking door*.
     ENTER MRS. PETTIBONE, *door* L. 3.   ALFRED *crosses
     at back over to* R., *and sits* R. *of* R. *table*.

MRS. P. (*motioning back to* EMILY *outside* L. 3.   Wait until
I've spoken to him. (*Turns to* PETTIBONE.   *Down* L. *of*
PETTIBONE.)

PET. (L. C.).   Madam, I have discovered everything —
everything !

MRS. P. (L. ; *with a cheerful look at* SMYTHE, *who is up* C.).
Oh, I'm very glad he told you !   I hope you are satisfied
with my choice.

PET.   Satis — ! (*Stops in utter amazement*.)

MRS. P.   Yes.   Mr. Smythe is a most deserving young
man, and of a very good family.

PET. (*becoming wild*).   What in the devil's name do I care
for his family !

MRS. P. (L.).   Have you any objection to him ?

PET. (L. C. ; *with scathing irony*).   Oh — not at all — not at all. And the other (*looks at* BENDER, R.), how about his family?

MRS. P. What other?

PET. Allow me. (*Takes* MRS. PETTIBONE *by the hand rather roughly, and leads her up to* BENDER, *who rises, and stands surprised* L. *of* R. *table.*) [McSNATH *is near* BENDER. Here is the other! Quite a gathering of your agreeable friends!

BEND. (*having risen ; politely to* PETTIBONE). May I beg the honor of an introduction?

PET. (C.). You mean to say you don't know my wife?

> [*Slight pause. All quiet.* McSNATH *comes down to* R. *of* PETTIBONE.

McSN. (*low but earnest voice*). Look here! Is that your wife? [*READY* EMILY *to enter* L. 3 E.

PET. (*looking at* MRS. PETTIBONE). Certainly.

> [McSNATH *gives one look, then turns abruptly about, and walks off at door up* R. *rapidly. Others watch* EXIT *of* McSNATH *up* R. D.

(*Turning to* MRS. PETTIBONE.) Rosabelle — how am I to explain your presence here?

MRS. P. (L.). Very simply. I took advantage of your absence in Hamburg —

PET. (L. C.). Ahem! (*Bus.*)

MRS. P. — to come here with Emily and bring about an understanding between her and Mr. Smythe (*indicating* SMYTHE, *who is up* C.), who have loved each other a long time, but were afraid to speak to you.

PET. (*after looking at* SMYTHE, *etc.*). Rosabelle — you will forgive me — I have been behaving like a lunatic — because I thought that he —

MRS. P. Yes — I know.

> [PETTIBONE *goes up and shakes hands with* SMYTHE. MRS. PETTIBONE *goes up with him.*

EMILY (*peeping out at door* L. 3). I can come now, can't I?

[*READY* Evangeline *and* Josephine, *to enter up*
R. *and* R. 3 E.

Mrs. P. Yes — yes.

[Emily *ENTERS at door* L. 3, *and goes quickly to*
Smythe, C. *Bus.* Pettibone *kisses her, etc.*

Pet. (*comes down; to* Alfred). But wait. Wait, I say.
How about Alfred?

Alf. (*seated* R.). Yes — you've overlooked me entirely.
(*Rises to* C.).

[Emily, Mrs. Pettibone, *and others looking on.*

Pet. (L. C.). You — you were going to marry her, weren't
you? [*READY* Tom, *to enter up* R.

Alf. (R. C.; *pulls out the paper used in Act* 1). That is
my impression. And this little document you signed just
before you left, will answer very well in a law-suit.

Pet.
Mrs. P. } Law-suit! Mercy on us! Dear me! (*Etc.*)
Emily

[Smythe *and* Emily C., *cross and go down* R.

Alf. But on the whole, I'll let it go, and resign myself to
my fate. (*Crosses back, meeting* Smythe *and* Emily; *shakes
hands and congratulates them both, and up round to* C.)

Bend. (*seated* L. *of* R. *table*). Yes — and the reason is, if
you'll permit me to speak, that his fate is to become my
son-in-law. [*The* Pettibone *family surprised.*

Mrs. P. (L.). Ah — this noble resignation!

ENTER Evangeline, *door up* R. *As she comes on,*
Josephine *ENTERS, door* R. 3, *meeting her* R.
On Josephine's *entrance,* Bender *rises and stands
stiffly and unmoved.*

Jos. (L. C.). Evangeline, I will go to the hotel —

Evan. (*up* R. C.). Mamma! (*Stopping her, and indicating
the gathering in the room.*)

Alf. (*going up for bus.*). Mrs. Bender, Evangeline — my
uncle, my aunt, my cousin, and Mr. Smythe. (*Bus.*)

ENTER Tom, *door up* R., *running in with great noise and slam, so that all look around.*

Tom (*to* C.). Mrs. Bender ! Mrs. Bender ! I've got that there lawyer fur ye at last. He's comin' up the steps. (Tom *stops up stage, looking at the crowd.*)

ALF. (*up* L. C. ; *entreatingly*). Ah — Mrs. Bender — be merciful !

EVAN. (*up* R. C. ; *with feeling*). Mamma — think of papa — think of us all.

> [JOSEPHINE, *up* C., *looks at* BENDER. *She begins to smile as if her stern resolve were melting.* BENDER *still stands rigid.* JOSEPHINE *comes down to* BENDER.

JOS. Theodore —

BEND. (R. *of* JOSEPHINE). I'm dead !

JOS. (L. *of* BENDER). That depends upon me. Theodore.

BEND. Do you think of resurrecting me ?

JOS. For the children's sake, I do

BEND. Then I forgive you.

> [JOSEPHINE *sits in chair* L. *of* R. *table,* BENDER *kneeling a little to* L. *of her ; simpering forgiveness, etc.*
>
> *MUSIC. Bright and catchy bit to end piece. Play* pp. *until cue "I Gits Half." Then forte for curtain.*

PET. (L.). Look here, Alfred, how in the world did all this come about — eh ?   [MRS. PETTIBONE L., EMILY R.

MRS. P. *and* EMILY (*together*). Yes — how was it ? We'd like to know.   [*READY Curtain.*

ALF. (C. ; *seizing* TOM *and bringing him down on his* L.). Through a little idea of mine in which I was ably assisted by taking this young man into partnership on the sole condition —

TOM. That I gits half.   [*RING Curtain.*

CURTAIN.

www.ingramcontent.com/pod-product-compliance
Lightning Source LLC
Chambersburg PA
CBHW020755020726
47495CB00008B/2436